Moonlight Shadow

Sabine Giebken

Translated by Karen Nickel Anhalt

Moonlight Shadow

Chapter 1

Colorful autumn leaves blew through the air as the two bicycles braked abruptly. The bicycle path ended there at a fork in the road.

Lena put down one foot and leaned on the handlebars. She was wearing her favorite sweater that was made of thick wool, a souvenir from Iceland. A strong gust of wind tousled her dark hair and blew apart her braid. She watched with amusement as her friend Britta pulled up her collar against the chill.

"Wow, what a wind! If it keeps up like this we can just fly home."

"I'm freezing to death already." Britta's teeth chattered. "It's just the right weather for doing math homework. Inside."

Lena stuck her nose into the wind and for a moment she closed her eyes with pleasure.

"Mmm, it smells so fresh! As if someone had thrown open a window to let fresh air into the entire world!"

"Did you drink silly juice at breakfast, or something?" Britta shook her head and smiled at her friend.

Lena opened her eyes again. "Hey, don't tell me you've forgotten what today is?"

"Thursday." Britta thought for a moment. "Hmm. Oh, yeah – Horse Day! Okay then."

Lena smiled. "Exactly! You know – On a horse's back nothing looks black. Or something like that."

Britta made a face and blew a strand of blonde hair out of her face.

"At least you don't have to ride in the woods on a chilly day like today."

"No, today we have training in the riding hall. Unfortunately. I love trotting through the newly fallen leaves!"

"Sure, that must be fun," Britta mumbled quietly.

For a moment Lena looked embarrassed. "I'm sorry. I always forget that it isn't fair to go on and on about how much I enjoy my riding lessons."

"It's not your fault that my mother won't let me go riding." Britta shrugged her shoulders and pulled her arms all the way into her sleeves. "But at least someone understands how I feel."

Lena looked at her friend sympathetically. Britta's father was no longer alive and her overprotective mother was afraid of animals and wouldn't allow her only daughter to take riding lessons. The only thing Britta could do about it was to read anything and everything she could get her hands on about horses and riding.

"Would you rather not come to the stable today?"

Britta smiled sadly. "No, I really want to. It's a lot better than just looking at horses in books!"

Lena hopped on one leg because her foot had fallen asleep. "Hey, I have to get going – my mother probably has my lunch waiting for me! Meet you in half an hour?"

"Usual place!" Britta slipped her hand back out of her cuffs and grabbed onto the handlebars. "See you later!"

Lena waved goodbye and watched her friend ride away. It was really unfair, she thought. *Britta is as crazy about horses as I am but she has to pass up on everything.* Lena couldn't imagine anything as horrible as sitting in the stands and watching everyone else learning to ride. *We have to do something to change that*, she thought.

"Would you like me to drive you to your riding lesson later?" asked Mrs. Bergman as she set a pot of steaming spaghetti on the table.

"No need. Britta's coming and we're walking over with Baloo." Lena quickly fished a few spaghetti strands out of the pot. Her little brother Larry tried to do the same, but he was too slow. Mrs. Bergman returned to the table and looked at him sternly.

"Larry, take some and put it on your plate. We don't eat straight out of the pot."

"But Lena did it too ..." Larry tattled immediately, but Mrs. Bergman simply shook her head.

"Say," she turned to her daughter, "you've already spent half the day together in school. Can't you bear to be apart for just a few hours? I thought Britta wasn't allowed to ride."

"She's allowed to watch. Which is better than nothing at all."

"I'll bet she rides secretly." Larry asserted boldly.

"That's not true at all! You have to have permission from your parents in order to take lessons!" Lena stuck her tongue out at her little brother. He couldn't know it, but he was partially right – after lessons were over, Lena gave her friend the horse to ride as he cooled down and nobody at the riding school had a problem with that.

Britta lived on the same street, just at the other end. Lena thought that was pretty great because it meant that they could go to school together every day, usually on their bikes. The only time they walked was in the winter, when the snow made the streets slick and icy and they had to be careful with every step they took.

Behind the last row of houses, there was a long field with a path that led to the woods. Lena took her dog Baloo off the leash and began to run when she saw that

8

Britta was already at their meeting point, a big white birch tree halfway between their houses, waiting for her.

"I couldn't find my riding boots," Lena rasped. "I bet Larry used them again to play cowboy."

Britta laughed and scratched the dog behind his ears as he joyfully jumped up on her to greet her. His muddy paws left brown prints on her jacket.

Baloo was a charcoal colored mutt. Lena and her parents had found him on the way home from a vacation, tied to a garbage can at a highway rest stop. The little fellow was about six months old at the time. Ever since then, Baloo had been a member of the family. The veterinarian had told them that he was a cross between a Labrador and a sheepdog, but no one really knew for sure. Baloo didn't care as long as everyone who heard the story of the poor little abandoned dog felt sorry for him and gave him a lot of love. He was good-hearted and friendly, but he seemed to live in permanent fear of being abandoned again. Whenever they had to tie him up in front of a store that didn't allow dogs, he would get so upset that he would howl like a wolf.

"Your brother is a real pain, huh?"

"Terrible. He's constantly trying to copy everything I do, and if he can't he tattles on me to my mother. His new thing is to burst into my room to find out what I do when my door is closed. That drives me crazy!"

A wide, pebbly path snaked through the woods and

led directly to the small town's riding school on the other side. "Come one, we're going to take a little detour past the garden."

She and Britta loved to zigzag through the woods, always discovering new ways to walk through. In the summer they'd picnic in the mossy clearings; in the winter they'd stand under the snow-covered pines and pretend that they had landed in enchanted fairy tale woods, as in the "Narnia" books. On a fall day like today, it was especially fun to leave the main path and stomp along the narrow side paths, where they were up to their ankles in rustling leaves. Lost in thought, Lena kicked a pinecone out of the way and Baloo jumped after it, like a cat chasing a mouse.

"It's about time something really exciting happened to us."

Britta chuckled and looked at her friend. "What do you have in mind?"

"Well, we could find a box filled with money! Money ... mysterious ... because it's hush money for a crime ... and the person who got it stuffed it in the box and buried it in the woods because he couldn't live with himself for having taken it."

Britta laughed. "Stuff like that only happens in very bad movies, Lena!"

"Just think about it. If we had money we could buy two horses for ourselves and then explore our woods on horseback!"

10

Baloo dropped the pinecone in front of Lena's feet and looked at her expectantly, his tail wagging happily.

"Great," Britta said sarcastically. "I could have my own horse and not be able to ride it. Or not be allowed to," she added and sighed. She picked up Baloos's spit-covered pinecone and threw it into the woods in a high arc. The dog chased after it enthusiastically.

"Oh, I'd be able to teach you," Lena mumbled and turned onto a narrow trail.

"Besides, we have no idea how much work two horses would be. Have you mucked out a stable before?"

"Nah, that's not something you learn at the riding school."

"But you should," maintained Britta. "Otherwise people buy themselves horses and think all they have to do with them is to ride them a little every day. Horses are a lot of work."

"Mucking out stables, feeding the horses, currying them – that's not what I'd call *work*!" Lena gave her dog a stern look and ignored the tattered pinecone that lay at her feet again. "You know, I'd really like to learn all that: what it's like when the blacksmith comes, what to do if a horse is sick, and everyday things like feeding and mucking. But in the riding school we're not allowed to do any of that because of the stupid insurance."

"You know what?" Britta said reflectively. "My mother won't let me ride, but she hasn't forbidden me from doing all the other stuff."

Baloo had given up on his pinecone and now strode along the fence, which was barely visible between the tall pine trees. He'd been the one to discover the garden in the middle of the woods one day; he had been sniffing around in the brush when he'd suddenly walked into the partially hidden fence links and barked loudly to register his annoyance. Lena had to smile every time she thought about how angry he had been at the obstruction. They had come back many times since then, driven by their curiosity. They wanted nothing more than to know what lay hidden in the middle of the garden, but they couldn't see in through the thick spruce and pine trees.

"Come on, let's walk past the gate. If someone's been here, we would see signs of it on the chain." Britta walked ahead and fished a crunched up piece of paper out of her pants pocket. She stopped when she reached the wrought iron gate and compared her sketch with the rusty chain that was wrapped three times around the jamb. "Nothing's changed," she said with disappointment and stuck the piece of paper back into her pocket.

Behind the gate, they could see a narrow path. After a few feet it made a sharp curve that made it impossible to see any further into the garden. Lena crooked her neck as far as she could and asked herself for the hundredth time what it was that the woods hid.

"I remember my mother used to take me for walks in the woods when I was real little. One time we came this

way; I can still remember it, because we noticed that a car was parked here, right in the middle of the woods. When we got a little closer, this old woman suddenly appeared. Her face was full of wrinkles like an old hag, but she smiled at us and gave me a four-leaf clover that she had just found. She chatted a while with my mother, then she limped off with her walking stick and went back into her garden. I still have the four-leaf clover, by the way. I dried it between pages of my horse dictionary."

Britta smiled when Lena finished. "Maybe the garden belonged to that old woman and now she's dead and no one takes care of it anymore."

"We should talk to someone official down at town hall. Someone has to know something about it."

"Hmm."

"What?"

"I'd much rather know what it looks like in the garden."

"We could ask."

"Don't you think we should just go in and take a look around?"

Lena looked around awkwardly. "You mean, break in?" The mere thought of it sent a shiver down her spine.

"No one has been in there in ages."

"Still, it would be trespassing."

"Well, okay, then let's break in."

"And what if someone sees us? This time of year there are a lot of people out walking in the woods."

14

"If we're fast no one will notice us. Come on, or are you chicken?"

"No way, of course not – but what are we going to do with Baloo? He can't climb over the fence with us, and you know what kind of a scene he makes whenever he's tied up." Relieved to have found an excuse, Lena stroked her dog's soft coat with a protective gesture. "Anyone coming by would think that he had been abandoned here in the middle of the woods ..."

Britta pensively looked at the fence between the trees.

"Oh, all right. Come on, let's get going – or you'll miss your riding lesson!"

The broad pebbled path led out of the woods down a gentle slope that was flanked on either side with expansive paddocks. A young mare at the far end briefly raised her head when Lena whistled to her, but didn't take the trouble to get any closer.

Sandra, Lena's riding instructor, sat on a bench, writing the names of her students onto a page in her notebook. Several girls waited around excitedly while Britta stood apart from them and scratched Baloo's soft, droopy ears. Lena crossed her fingers tightly and whispered under her breath, "Boomer, Boomer, Boomer."

"So, is everyone here now?" Sandra looked up at the group. "Okay then. Today we'll be working on dressage. We already tried out a few basic techniques last week and that went quite well. Today I'd like to try the same ones again, but this time each of you will ride a different horse."

Lena let out a disappointed moan. She had been allowed to ride her favorite horse last week. But maybe Sandra had forgotten that.

"Let's see, who did you have last time?" Sandra paged through her notebook. *Darn it*, thought Lena. "Julia, you did quite well with Jasper. Today Ellie will give him a try and Julia will be riding Boomer. Lena, I'd like to see you on Katja today. You know she can be a little lazy, but with the right guidance she can do all the movements."

"But she's so boring," Lena complained. Ellie gave her a sympathetic look and Julia grinned spitefully.

"You should see it as a challenge," Sandra admonished her with her eyebrows raised. "If you do a good job with these movements on Katja, then maybe I'll let you ride Boomer again next week."

With a long face, Lena set off to fetch the huge chestnut mare from her box. Katja was so big that Lena had to stretch out her arm just to touch her pronounced withers, the highest part of the horse's body. Despite her impressive size the mare was gentle and excellent to ride, except for the fact that she had already reached a ripe old age and knew all the movements by heart, so even a beginner had an easy time riding her.

Lena turned her head and looked longingly at the

young gelding tied up over at the stable wall, impatiently scratching the ground with his fore hoof. Boomer had been participating in riding lessons for only a few months. His gaits were wonderfully soft and you could signal him with the slightest cue because he wasn't yet as worn out as so many of the school horses, who had been used for lessons year in and year out. You needed a lot of equestrian skill and really had to concentrate for the entire hour-long lesson in order to master all of the movements with him, but that was exactly what made it fun and exciting. Aside from that, he had big gentle eyes and every time you curried him he would playfully try to snatch the brush away. Lena loved the dark brown gelding more than anything.

"Julia has been here for an hour already," Ellie whispered as she tied up Jasper next to Katja. "She helped curry Sandra's horse and braid its mane for the tournament Sandra is entered in tomorrow."

"Somebody obviously did quite a job brown-nosing around here," murmured Lena. "No wonder she got to ride Boomer."

The never-ending battles with Julia, who was the same age as she, had slowly but surely gotten on Lena's nerves. Julia was very popular and most of the other girls admired her riding skills and hovered around her constantly. If there was a new horse, or a horse that was especially difficult, they always called in Julia. She enjoyed being the center of attention and being thought of as the best student. Ever since young Boomer began participating in lessons, Julia fought to ride him as often as possible.

"I'll bet she doesn't even care about Boomer. She just wants him because she can show off with him."

"For her to give up Boomer voluntarily, Sandra would have to buy a fantastic new horse for lessons," Ellie complained. She and Julia didn't particularly like each other because to Ellie riding was nothing more than another fun activity. "An expensive, incredible horse that no one else could handle."

Lena dragged the saddle out of the tack room and groaned until she finally managed to heave it onto Katja's back. "Getting the saddle up there is one thing," she said, shaking her head as she pulled the girth tight. "But I have to get up there, too."

Ellie led Jasper into the covered riding arena alongside Lena. "Just look at Julia acting like a big shot. Now she's even gotten herself running reins."

Sandra stood in the center next to Boomer and explained to his rider what she had to remember when using running reins. Julia nodded. She was antsy. As she rode past Lena, Boomer chomped indignantly on his bit and tossed his head back and forth as if he were trying to get rid of the unfamiliar pressure on his mouth.

Sandra clapped her hands once. Boomer was startled

and jumped. Baloo barked enthusiastically from up in the spectator stands and the gelding jumped again.

"Would it be very mean to laugh if she goes flying off the horse?" Ellie chuckled.

"Everyone take up the reins and start trotting! Careful with Boomer, Julia – yes, that's good. Give him more slack at first so that he can get used to the reins. Lena, a little more action, or Katja will fall asleep while she's walking."

Lena broke into a sweat in no time. Katja reminded her of an unwieldy truck, stiffly careening around the corner. With determination, she tried to guide the mare by squeezing her legs and bending her around her inside leg in the corners. When she had no energy left, she switched on the second hoof beat and slowed down to a walk.

"I can't get her to loosen up," she whined dejectedly. "She slogs around like Santa Claus walking through a snowdrift."

Sandra had to laugh. "Come now, it doesn't look half that bad. In her own way Katja is difficult to ride – she doesn't pull any tricks like a young horse, but you have to be a good equestrian in order to ride school figures accurately with her. Ride down here on the circle and try to bend her in more."

Lena tried it until Sandra was satisfied. The next problem was the canter – Katja was clearly of the opinion that she had done enough for the day and simply refused to canter. Lena needed two long sides before she finally managed it.

Ellie cantered Jasper on the wrong lead. "Try it in the corner, Ellie, and bend him in more," Sandra suggested. Ellie obeyed and Jasper jumped in a dreadful, disjointed canter. "Stop! That won't do at all. Ride a circle and then strike off again."

Sandra was exasperated because Ellie was laughing so hard that she nearly fell off her horse. "Did you see that?" she gasped. "To be able to run like that without all four feet getting tangled? Amazing!"

After Ellie finally succeeded, it was Julia's turn. Boomer struck off picture-perfect and used the long side to do a few frisky buck kicks. Lena watched the gelding closely and wished desperately that she could be sitting on his back.

Sandra was satisfied with them. "Very good, Julia, he's really doing great."

When the lesson was over, Lena jumped off her horse and helped Britta climb into the saddle. Considering that her friend had never had a professional riding lesson, she sat very confidently in the saddle. Lena hurried over to the stands to Baloo who, as usual, hung his front paws over the railing and observed everything closely.

"How lucky that you got Katja, so your friend could ride without someone leading the horse." Julia brought Boomer to a stop directly next to the stands and smiled as she patted his sweaty neck. "And it's better for Boomer not to have so many different riders. Especially since he's still in training and has to learn to respond to the reins."

"Are you trying to tell me I'm not capable of riding him?" Lena retorted angrily and pointed to the running reins.

Julia shrugged her shoulders. "Someone who couldn't even get Katja to canter ..."

"Then why don't you ride her, if you're so sure you can do it better."

Julia looked down at her from on top of the horse and smiled haughtily. "You just practice on the old school horses first and leave the more challenging horses to me. By the way, Sandra said that I ride Boomer very well. Which means that I'll surely be riding him more often from now on." With that, she cued the gelding and rode off in a leisurely fashion.

Lena watched her go and boiled with anger. It just wasn't fair! Why did Boomer have to be trained on the running reins today of all days?

Britta joyfully dismounted the horse and insisted on leading the mare to the saddling area, exchanging the bridle for the simple halter she wore in the stable. By now, she was nearly as skilled as Lena at completing that task.

"That was so excellent – thank you so so, so much!" Britta's eyes shone with excitement and Lena had to laugh. *What the heck*, she thought. *At least I'm allowed to take riding lessons*. She felt sorry for Britta, because she could only watch the others for the entire hour. What was giving up a few minutes of being on the horse, cooling it down, in comparison?

"I'm happy that I can do that for you," said Lena, and she truly meant it. Together they took care of Katja and Lena brought her back to her box. Ellie waved a happy goodbye as they left. "See you next week!" Lena took Baloo off his leash so that he could have some fun after all that waiting.

Britta cheered her up a few times on the way back. "Hey, you don't have to feel bad because of me, okay? Look, if it weren't for you, I'd never even get close to a horse!"

"Your mother is so unfair," Lena blurted out. "You know what we're going to do? We'll tie her up, bring her to a horse stable and lock her in a box. Then we'll leave her there until she finally lets you ride!"

Britta had to laugh. "Then I'll be an orphan, because she would probably die of fear!"

"We'll figure something out. You'll learn all about riding – cantering, galloping and everything that goes with it. I promise!"

When they reached the birch tree, Britta took Baloo's head in her hands and scratched his floppy ears to say goodbye. "Okay, but not until I'm eighteen and my mother can't forbid me to do it anymore."

When Lena got back home from the stable, she tossed her riding boots into the guest bathroom and hungrily grabbed a freshly baked cookie from the kitchen. While she was chewing, her cell phone rang.

"Hullo," Lena mumbled between bites of the cookie.

"Hey, it's me! Listen up: meet me tonight at our usual spot." Britta lowered her voice. "We're going into the garden tonight!"

Lena choked on her cookie and had a coughing fit.

"You want to go into the woods at night? Have you gone crazy? It'll be pitch black!"

"Don't be afraid, I'll bring a flashlight along. But leave Baloo home!"

Lena hung up and shook her head. She fed the rest of her cookie to Baloo, who had carefully observed every bite she had taken.

"Well, Baloo, if I don't come back again, at least you'll know where to look for me."

Chapter 2

The horse couldn't see clearly. Its eyes were wide open, but all it saw up ahead was fog. The horse's body didn't cooperate either; whenever it tried to turn its head, it seemed to have forgotten where it wanted to go. The horse couldn't remember ever having been this helpless before.

But there was something worse than the feeling of helplessness: the feeling of fear. The stallion was extremely sensitive and his natural instinct told him that danger lurked. Great danger. Unconsciously, the stallion whinnied. It seemed like he was calling for help, as if he were trying to tell someone that he was in danger but couldn't move. But before the horse could whinny again, the world around him sank back into a thick fog.

The thing that couldn't be seen by the horse's eyes, but which the animal's sensitive ears picked up as if in a dream, was an eerie crackling and hissing noise, a sound that could only come from one thing; fire. The wispy flames had already devoured the straw and begun to climb up the brittle wooden walls. The wood was old and there hadn't been any rain for a long time. In a flash, the horse was surrounded by the flames.

Something stirred deep down inside the sensitive animal. It was a battle – a battle that the stallion could win only with his powerful will. He fought his way through the fog and managed to toss his head from side to side.

Heat. It was so unbearably hot that the air itself seemed to be on fire. The stallion's will to survive became overpowering. With a formidable jerk, he ripped the rusty hook to which his line was attached out of the wall.

Fire was everywhere. The horse spun around in panic. The flames had reached the ceiling and roof beams crashed loudly to the ground, opening up to the night sky. A tree that grew too close to the building caught fire as well.

Panic had cleared the fog and the horse could finally see clearly. Over there – there was an opening between the flames! Just at that moment, another beam crashed to the ground. It landed on the stallion's croup and singed his coat and tail. But the horse took no notice.

Much too small. The opening in the flames was much too small! But the air inside was getting thin. The air that the horse so desperately needed to breathe. He tensed his muscles and assessed the distance. Then, like black lightning, the stallion shot through the flames. Cold, clear night air filled his lungs. He had been injured, but that didn't matter to him. He was alive. That was the only thing that counted.

The fire had spread to several trees and would continue to spread quickly. A thick wall of heat rose up. The sound of the powerful flames crackling and popping was frighteningly loud in the horse's sensitive ears.

The stallion whinnied again. This time his voice was loud and clear. He was victorious. He had escaped. He was still alive.

Without looking back, the horse galloped off into the night.

It was pitch black when Lena looked out the window. She wasn't afraid of the dark, but the thought of walking through the woods right now did make her feel a little uneasy. Lena listened closely but the only thing she could hear was her own quiet breathing. With her Icelandic sweater under her arm, she slipped out of her room on her tiptoes.

Britta was already waiting for her at the birch tree. She had put on a black jacket so that she wouldn't be easy to see in the dark. She gave her friend a conspiratorial smile, and Lena pulled her lips into an uncertain grin.

"Are we really going to go through with it?"

"You're not going to back out now, are you Lena?"

"Noooo – but just imagine all the things that could be waiting for us in that garden ..."

"We'll never find out for sure if we don't finally take a look for ourselves."

Lena giggled nervously. She grabbed her friend's hand and together they quickly marched into the woods.

In the daytime, there was nothing at all spooky about the woods. On the contrary, Lena usually felt snug and secure, as if the dense pines were her second home. But things were very different in the night. The woods were suddenly filled with noises – owls screeched, the wind wailed through the treetops and made the tree branches creak and groan. Every time an animal rustled through the brush Lena tensed up and dug her fingers into Britta's sleeve.

"What was that?"

"Lena, be quiet, you're making me nervous."

"Let's turn around – please!"

"No way, we started this and we'll finish it!"

Lena closed her eyes tightly. She didn't want to see whatever spooky thing the thin beam from Britta's flashlight revealed next so she let her friend guide them along. She wished Baloo were with them.

Britta stayed on the wide path for a while, and then she turned off onto the path they had taken that afternoon. Without any warning, she came to a sudden stop and Lena walked into her.

"Ouch!"

"Sorry."

"It's not really all that spooky, is it?"

"I don't know, I haven't really been looking."

"Lena, open your eyes this minute!"

Lena obeyed and looked around carefully. If you looked closely, the woods were truly lovely. The trees glowed in the moonlight and every so often a star would twinkle through the tops of the pine trees. An owl shrieked again, but this time Lena thought the sound was more charming than frightening.

"Mmm, how peaceful it looks!"

Britta shook her head incredulously and gave her friend a shove.

"We've arrived. The gate is over there."

The girls looked at each other. Britta got down on her knees and felt along the bottom of the chain link fence for a loose spot. When she found one, she lifted the fence up and shimmied underneath it. She didn't seem to care that her jacket scraped along the ground and a mixture of the loamy woodland earth and autumn leaves stuck to it.

Lena took a deep breath and followed her friend. She felt her heart beating loudly. *We're doing something illegal. We're breaking into a stranger's property.* She quickly pushed those thoughts aside.

Once on the other side, she got up slowly and shook herself the way Baloo did when he came home after getting sopping wet on a rainy day. Leaves stuck to her Icelandic sweater and in her hair. She dashed off after Britta.

Her friend was already making her way down a narrow path that snaked through the trees and led deeper and deeper into the mysterious garden.

"Looks like a park!" Lena observed and looked around with her eyes wide open. The trees stood farther apart than they did in the rest of the woods.

"Look over here – what's this?" Britta had discovered a shed made of boards. Lena followed her and waited until she aimed the beam of her flashlight into the interior of the shed. Inside there was all sorts of junk: folding chairs, half a rake, two badminton racquets, a lumpy soccer ball and various gardening tools strewn across the makeshift shelves.

Britta shut the door and continued on. The path snaked over a small raised knob of earth and fed into a wider path that encircled a huge meadow. Britta stopped so abruptly that Lena walked into her again.

"Now take a look at that! It's like an illustration out of a fairy tale book!" Britta gaped.

They stood before a clearing bathed in slivery moonlight. All around the path leafy trees and pines shielded the meadow from view. The only way to see it was to stand right in front of it.

And it really did look like something out of a fairy tale.

Underneath the open sky stretched the most beautiful garden that Lena had ever seen in her life. White marble statues guarded a magnificent lagoon in the center of the enclosure and, although the trees surrounding it had withered long ago, the view reminded her of a palace garden.

"Wow!" Lena was impressed. "That is just totally crazy. Do you suppose all this belonged to that old lady?"

"One thing's for sure, no one has taken care of it in a long time. It sure looks like it's gone wild."

Britta was right – green moss grew on the statues and the grass grew past her ankles. If you looked closely you could see that it was being choked by weeds.

"Maybe she didn't have any children to inherit the garden."

"Just think about it; it doesn't belong to anyone any more. Maybe *we* could take care of it?"

Suddenly Lena couldn't bear to stand still any longer. It was as if she didn't want to be an observer anymore, but wanted to be a part of this strange world under the sparkling starry sky. She ran into the garden. With her arms stretched out wide, she spun around in a circle in the middle of the meadow, laid her head back and let out a wolf's howl. Then in full voice she sang off-key the old song her mother used to sing to her, "Carried away by a moonlight shadow ..."

Britta stood there and laughed. Then she too ran into the center of the park and contemplated the night sky.

"I feel as if I'm hooked on the woods. I'm staying here!"

"If we were to bring enough to eat, then we could stay here a few days, don't you think?"

"And we could fix everything up again. I can already picture it: water lilies in the lagoon, colorful flowers all around, and us lying in the grass, sunbathing. And we'd replace all the statues with bronze horses."

"Bronze horses – forget it! *Real* horses! Everywhere!"

Lena mimicked a whinny and then galloped wildly across the meadow. Then she let herself fall into the grass, exhausted. Britta joined her and sat down next to her friend.

"Nobody will believe us! A fairy tale park in the middle of the woods!"

Lena closed her eyes. The silence surrounded them. Not a single cricket chirped, because they disappeared in the warm summer months. Instead, the air was wonderfully cold and clear. She opened her eyes again and looked at the starry night sky. *A bed made of grass and a blanket of stars*, she thought and giggled.

Britta stood up first. "Come one, we'd better get going. Before the dawn surprises us!"

They left the garden the same way that they had come. Britta carefully bent down the wire fence over the spot they had crawled under. It seemed to her that this little adventure had made them immune to fear.

It was strange, but now the woods didn't have anything spooky about them anymore. Lena sang to herself and Britta joined in cheerfully.

On a night like this, just about anything could happen, Lena thought with excitement.

Chapter 3

The junction to the path that led to the entrance of the woodland garden was just a few steps behind them when Britta stopped suddenly. She paused there and listed closely. "Did you hear that, too?" she whispered.

Lena shook her head and also listened closely. "What was it?" she whispered back.

"I don't know. But it sounded close by!"

A few feet ahead of them two deer suddenly broke out of the brush. Startled, the girls screamed and held on to each other tightly. The deer raced across the path and then disappeared in the opposite side of the woods. For a few heartbeats everything was silent. Then, a little further away, another pair of deer dashed through the woods.

Lena let go of her friend and laughed nervously.

"Deer! We were afraid of a pair of deer!"

Britta cocked her head to the side and listened in the direction that the animals had come from.

"Something must have startled them," she whispered.

"Maybe they were in the garden too and that's why they're so fired up!" Lena giggled again. But that was to cover up the fact that she was afraid.

"Shhh," said Britta.

The path they were standing on shimmered silvery in the moonlight. But the woods around them were black and dark. Not a single beam of light made it through the trees. It was impossible to make anything out. Every little sound seemed so much louder. *This must be what it's like when you're blind*, thought Lena. *If you could only rely on your ears.*

Three more deer broke out of the woods, this time further down the path. They also seemed agitated, as if they were fleeing from something, or someone.

The two friends looked at each other.

"I think we'd better get out of here," Britta murmured. "Whatever it is that startled the deer, it's coming closer to us – I can hear it!"

A distinct cracking sound came out of the darkness of the woods and proved that Britta was right. Lena grabbed her friend's arm and pulled her along. Another crack, louder this time, and closer. Lena was petrified now. She let go of Britta and began to run.

⌘　⌘　⌘　⌘

Then something big jumped out of the woods at the exact spot where the girls had been standing moments before.

Lena screamed and whipped around. The only thing behind them was the dark path, looking as innocent as a dark stream. *Are we both going crazy?* she thought. *But we both hear it!* Britta's breath came in gasps. Lena only now noticed that her friend had grabbed her sleeve and was holding on tight.

Silvery moonlight shone through the treetops and made patterns on the woodland ground, except for one spot further ahead. Over there it was so dark that it looked as if someone had turned off the light or used an eraser to remove part of the path. A dark shadow seemed to completely swallow the peaceful moonlight. Lena looked a little more closely. Was she dreaming, or had one of those shadows just moved?

"Britta, pass me the flashlight," she whispered quietly and forgot that she had just shrieked loudly.

Her friend reluctantly let go of Lena's sweater and felt around in her jacket pocket for the flashlight. Her trembling fingers felt around for the button to turn it on, but just as she found it, they heard a deep rumbling sound – coming from the direction of the shadow!

Britta was so frightened that she dropped the flashlight. She crouched down and felt around on the ground for it. As if on command, the moon disappeared behind a cloud, putting the entire scene into a spooky twilight. There! The shadow moved again, slinking slowly and fluidly toward them! Lena remained motionless as she stared at the strange creature. Her brain shouted to her, *run, run away as fast as you can!* but her legs didn't listen and simply refused the command. More strange sounds came from the shadow. Then it suddenly seemed to get bigger, to grow, and then collapse onto itself again. There was another loud thud and then the woodland floor shook under Lena's feet. Britta jumped to her feet, grabbed Lena's sleeve again and pulled her backwards.

In the very next moment, the clouds pulled away from the moon again. The shadow snorted again. Suddenly, a fist-sized eye glimmered in the weak moonlight. Normally Britta was the one to keep a cool head while Lena ran off shrieking, but this time she was the one to get hysterical. Britta screamed, turned in a circle, and then ran off blindly into the darkness.

Afterwards Lena couldn't explain what it was that kept her from running away, but she stood there rooted to the spot. Her breath came in bursts and cold sweat covered the back of her neck. Still something held her there. Was it the soft scratching sounds made by this creature in the dark that awakened a very specific memory in her? In those few minutes that decided everything, Lena didn't give any of it a thought. She didn't even feel especially courageous when she took a tentative stop forward; she acted impulsively, on a gut feeling.

The creature in the shadows continued moving in her direction. The closer it got, the longer it seemed to become until Lena was able to make out that it was stretching its neck ... its long, narrow neck ... with an elongated head, flared nostrils, pointy ears cocked in her direction. Lena took a deep breath.

In front of her stood a horse!

One snort and the spell was broken. Lena felt her breathing calm down. Her brain still didn't want to believe what her eyes were seeing. She took another step toward the horse, then another, and finally stopped and waited to see what would happen. Now that she knew what that thing was standing in front of her, she was no longer afraid. On the contrary, she felt butterflies in her stomach as she slowly stretched out her hand. A horse, here, in the middle of the woods!

The horse also stood quietly. He snorted and puffed as if he were trying to get a whiff of the person suddenly standing in front of him. Inch by inch, he moved his nose closer to her outstretched hand, stretching his neck longer and longer. His nostrils flared, scented, and he commanded his muscles to be on alert in case he had to run off in a flash.

The girl emanated an aura of calm. The horse no

longer sensed any of the fear and panic that had been in the air moments ago, and concluded that the danger had been banished. In front of him stood a normal person. Two determined steps and the stallion stood so close to the girl that his breath reached her face.

Lena had held her breath involuntarily and waited to see if the horse would trust her. She knew that she should avoid startling it with a sudden hand movement and stood very still even though her arm was feeling very heavy. When the horse came closer and puffed into her face, she smiled with relief. Then she dared to lift her hand in order to gently stroke its dark neck.

She had never seen such a breathtakingly beautiful horse. His black coat gleamed in the moonlight and felt like silk under her fingertips. He wasn't all that big, with a withers height at about eye level for her. But there was so much pride and confidence in his posture that he gave off the impression of being a giant. Lena's fingers glided almost reverently through the long, thick mane.

Suddenly the horse tensed all his muscles and pricked his ears. Lena carefully turned her head. She had an idea what it was that the horse had seen.

"Lena? Are you okay?"

Britta's voice sounded so thin and frightened that Lena practically had to bite her tongue to keep from laughing.

"I'm over here! Come on already, you coward. This monster's not going to eat you up!"

Reluctantly Britta came closer. She still couldn't see what the spooky shadowy creature really was.

"Who is that?"

"A tall dark stranger."

As if to confirm that, the horse let out a low rumbling sound. Britta shook and did not dare to come any closer.

"Shhh, you'll scare it off again," Lena whispered to the shadow. She noted with admiration that the horse didn't flee. He stood there full of self-confidence, looking at the stranger. Almost as if he wanted to protect her.

Lena heard Britta walk into the flashlight that she had dropped. In the moonlight, she saw her quickly bend over to pick up it up, as if that were what she needed to feel better. Lena concealed a smile when the beam of light shone in her direction, because Britta got another fright and dropped the flashlight again.

"But that's a horse!"

Lena laughed spiritedly. "I know! Can you believe it? Come here and take a closer look at him!" She felt the horse relax again as he puffed and flared his nostrils to get wind of Britta's aura.

"Wow, I can't believe it!" Britta's voice was hardly more than a whisper. She stopped a few feet away from the animal and carefully stretched out her hand, waiting until the soft horse nose touched her fingers.

"So buddy, what are you doing out here all alone?"

"Shooing deer," Lena observed dryly. And scaring innocent bystanders!"

"Look at this, there's a line hanging from his halter!" Britta took the loose end in her hand and looked over the hook to which it was still knotted. "He tore himself away!"

"Guess he wanted to take a nighttime walk in the woods too." Lena's voice had a dreamy undertone to it. She still couldn't believe what was happening!

"Oh wow. What are we going to do with him now?"

Lena ran her hand down the black horse's chest. *He's so muscular*, she thought with wonder, but then the animal flinched. "Hey, what's this?" She reached for the flashlight and illuminated the spot that her finger had just touched. "Take a look over here; it looks like he's missing a chunk of his coat."

"Lena, this is getting too creepy for me! First a horse suddenly appears in the middle of the night and now it's injured, too ..."

Lena laughed at her. "And what is so creepy about that?"

"Well, think about it for a minute – what injured him? Maybe he's running away and there's someone sneaking around here looking for him? I think we should get out of here right now."

"Don't worry," Lena shook her head and examined the rest of the horse's body with the flashlight. She discovered several other spots like the one on his chest, but couldn't make heads or tails of it. "If there were something dangerous running around here, then this fellow wouldn't be this placid," she mumbled. "Hey, do you smell that?"

Britta sniffed. "Smoke! Is that what he smells like?"

"A fire," said Lena thoughtfully. "That could be it! These are burns on his coat."

"That would mean that he probably fled from a burning stable!" Britta's voice trembled with agitation. "Oh my goodness, the poor animal!"

Lena stroked his velvety neck and said a few comforting words to the horse. "We can't just leave him here, can we?"

"Hmm. At any rate, we need to find his owner. But that shouldn't be too difficult. If a stable really did burn down, then there will probably be a story about it in the newspaper."

"And until then, he'll live with me at my house; that's something I've always wished for!" Lena had to giggle, as she tried to imagine her mother's face when she looked out of the window the next morning and discovered a horse in her beloved flowerbed.

"I have a much better idea," Britta said. "What would you say to having your very own beautiful garden, in the middle of the woods, and it's all yours?" she asked the black horse, who looked at her with his big eyes as if he understood each and every word.

"What? You want to leave him here? Are you crazy?"

"Do you have a better idea? Tomorrow we'll let him out again, but we can hardly go to our parents now and say, 'Hey folks, we took a walk in the woods in the middle of the night last night in order to trespass on someone else's property, and while we were at it we found this horse!' I'd be under house arrest until I turn eighteen."

Lena thought it over. How she wished she could take the horse home with her! But Britta was right. Their nighttime outing would be hard to explain. "Alright, then. But how are we going to get him in there? He won't exactly fit under the fence."

"Very funny. I'll go back in there and take a look and see if I can find anything useful among all the gardening tools in that shed."

Lena reached for the lead that still hung from the halter. She gingerly took a few steps and the black horse followed her obediently.

For the second time that night she waited for Britta in front of the gate to the woodland garden, but this time she had to pinch herself in the arm to reassure herself that the beautiful black horse next to her wasn't just a mirage.

"Hah!" Britta returned with giant hedge shears, which she used to cut the chain that had been wrapped around the two gateposts for an endlessly long time. On the inside they were completely rusted. She bowed, and then opened the gate to allow Lena and the horse to enter.

"Now you can finally throw away your sketch of the

chain," Lena grinned. "We'll have to buy another lock, and then we'll be the only ones who can go into the garden."

They followed the path to the clearing that lay hidden behind the pine trees. Lena sighed heavily and then removed the lead from the horse's halter and watched as he took broad strides to inspect his new surroundings. With his head held high and his ears pricked, he trotted across the sweeping meadow, disappearing between the trees and then reappearing before finally stopping in the middle to bathe in the moonlight with his gaze fixed upon the girls. Lena held her breath reverently. What an enchanting view; precisely how she had pictured it an hour ago in her dreams.

"I have a feeling he likes it here," Britta whispered. "Take a look; he discovered the lagoon. At least he'll have enough to eat and drink here."

Lena nodded absently, completely consumed by the moment. The silvery moonlight was reflected in the water and in the shimmering eyes of the black horse, and Lena was certain that she had never seen anything this beautiful in her entire life.

"What are you thinking?" Britta asked as she eyeballed her with amusement.

Instead of an answer, Lena quietly hummed a melody for her and the words slipped out of her mouth as if the moon has just whispered them to her; "Moonlight Shadow!"

Chapter 4

Never before had a school day lasted as long as it did the next day. When the bell finally rang at the end of the last class, Lena and Britta jumped up and were out the door before their teacher could finish her last sentence. On the way home Lena felt as if they had set a new speed record, considering how incredibly out of breath she was when they got to the end of the bike path.

"Okay, I'll zip home for lunch and then I'll bring Baloo, or else my mother will just ask a lot of unnecessary questions."

"Bring along some ointment," Britta called over her shoulder. "One for animals, so we can treat his wounds."

Lena saluted jokingly and got back on her bicycle. "I'll be at our meeting point in half an hour!" she called, and then she furiously pedaled home. She was about as excited as she had been right before her first riding lesson and everything in her head was swirling around one single thought; *Is it really true, did we really find a horse?*

"What, you're home already? Is Britta sick today?"

"Nah – we're meeting up again right away. I just want to quickly get Baloo and then ..."

"One moment, young lady; first you'll be eating your lunch. It's not quite ready yet; I wasn't expecting you this early."

Lena groaned. She knew that her mother would never let her leave the house without having lunch. Baloo came along with a happy "Woof!" behind her brother, walking out of the adjoining living room. He jumped up on her excitedly.

"Hi there, little Baloo. So, do you want to come along today?"

"Where are you guys going?" asked Larry, who was curious.

"None of your business."

"Don't be so rude to your brother!" Mrs. Bergman called out sternly from the kitchen.

Boy, if he only knew what we were planning to do! But Lena was wise enough to keep her mouth shut. If she talked back and start arguing with her mother, she'd wind up having to take Larry with her. Instead she reached for the newspaper on the table and scanned the local headlines.

"I'm starting to worry about you," joked Mrs. Bergman, as she set a steaming plate down on the table between her children. "No endless chat with Britta today, and now you're even reading the newspaper – what do you think, Larry, should we take her to the doctor?"

Lena made a face. "Ha, ha. In school I heard that a stable burned down last night somewhere in our area – did you hear anything about it?" she asked as casually as possible.

Mrs. Bergman shook her head. "A stable? No. It probably wasn't really in our area, or there would have been a story about it. Hey, start eating!"

Baloo got caught up in Lena's rush. He scurried around her legs as she quickly dashed upstairs to look for the ointment. Then, ever inquisitive, he followed her into the garage where Lena hastily rummaged around in Mr. Bergman's toolbox until she had found her old bicycle lock. She pilfered two apples out of the box of slightly bruised apples intended for the stable horses. Then she jogged quickly to the meeting spot where Britta was already waiting.

The sun shone brightly when they reached the narrow path that led along the fence to the entrance of the woodland garden. Baloo walked ahead, sniffing along the way, and Lena watched him intently to see if he would scent the horse.

"My dog isn't aware of the new resident yet," she noted

after a while, with some disappointment when she saw Baloo's boredom. He picked up a stick and dragged it along.

"I don't hear a thing. Do you suppose it ran off?

"Oh, come on," said Lena. "Since when can you hear a horse standing on a meadow, grazing?"

Britta giggled. "My tummy feels like I swallowed a whole flock of birds!"

The gate looked the same as it always did. One had to look very closely to see that the chain now had two broken links. Lena unwrapped it from the posts and pushed open the gate. Thrilled, Baloo pushed past her, but thanks to the stick in his mouth he got caught in the chain link fence and couldn't go forward or backward.

"Silly dog!" Lena quickly attached the leash to his collar and pulled him back. He refused to give up the stick. Britta was already walking down the narrow path to the clearing by the time Lena finally managed to maneuver Baloo into the garden and to close the gate and lock it with the chain.

"Don't you go making a racket in here, Baloo – understand?"

In the daylight, the garden looked completely different from how it had looked the previous night. In the moonlight it had been wild and romantic, but by day it just looked unkempt and shabby. Still, it wasn't the garden they were interested in at the moment, Lena thought to herself as she felt the pins and needles come back.

Baloo pulled like crazy on his leash, and it was all Lena could do to slow him down because her hands were damp with sweat. Had the dog finally realized that there was something else here or had he simply been infected by all their excitement?

When they reached the last curve, Lena held her breath in anticipation. Before them was the park-like meadow, but it was as deserted as it had been the first time they visited it.

When the horse had woken up in the morning he had felt strange. On the one hand, his lungs still ached from all the smoke that he had breathed the previous night. And then there were all the bruises and wounds in his coat that still burned, as if the fire were still there. On the other hand, for the first time in his life, he felt alive.

The stallion had forgotten how wonderful it was to wake up with the sky over his head. At home, he had lived in a spacious box in a stable. Sometimes he felt that he was going to burst with all the energy he built up, and when it was time for training he couldn't run enough to burn it all up. But here it was different. Last night he had galloped a few times around the meadow, just for the fun of it. His legs had felt wonderfully tired and calm. The need to run had eventually dispersed, and he had had the best night's sleep since his days as a foal.

Early in the morning he had awakened, looked around

sleepily, and closed his eyes again to doze a little longer.
No clattering feed pail to tear him out of his dreams and
no cranky stable hand to chase him from one corner of
the box to the next with a pitchfork. After a while, when
the first rays of sunshine warmed his coat, he wandered
around the meadow and picked at a few blades of grass.
This new life was so wonderful that he had hardly
noticed the time passing.

The stallion knew that he had his own powerful will
to thank for this new life. No one would have saved him
from the fire if he hadn't done it himself. And no one
could have forced him to follow the two girls later if he
alone hadn't decided to trust them. Now he spied the
two of them on the edge of the meadow. He observed
them for a while from the shadows of the trees. Then he
decided that he could still trust them, and walked into
the sunlight.

Baloo saw the horse first. Indignant, he dropped his stick
and began to bark wildly.

Lena, startled, pulled him close to her and held his
muzzle closed with her hands.

"Baloo, cut the barking! You're going to give us away
– now be quiet!"

The horse didn't seem to be the least bit impressed
by the dog. Without rushing, he came closer and then
stopped in the middle of the meadow.

"Incredible," Lena whispered quietly. There it was, the horse of her dreams. Black and beautiful, with his head held high, he looked at her as if he had been waiting for her all his life. He had a small white star on his forehead, but beyond that no other marking disturbed his flawless coat. Lena could have stood there forever just staring at the black horse.

Baloo jerked and pulled his leash until Lena finally came back to life. When he reached a point about six feet from the stallion, the dog stopped and stayed rooted to the spot. He planted his paws firmly in the ground and refused to take another step. The girls looked at each other and smiled.

"I believe that my little Baloo will not be chasing any horses today!" Lena patted Baloo's head and detached the leash from his collar. Like a flash, the dog took off and disappeared behind a statue where, from a safe distance, he could peer out at the big black animal as it stretched its neck toward the girls.

Lena couldn't stay still a minute longer. With her heart pounding, she approached the black horse and gently blew in his nostrils. How soft his coat was! She stroked his neck, his back and his flanks, searching for burns, and found a few that looked quite serious. Concerned, she turned to Britta, but her friend shyly kept her distance. What was wrong? Was she afraid or something?

"Britta, take a look; he has a lot of these wounds, everywhere! There's a deep one up here on his back that must hurt like crazy!"

Lena could sense her friend's uncertainty, but Britta summoned her courage and approached, trying not to let it show. She gingerly stroked the black neck and even smiled when the horse puffed in her face.

"Take a look; this is what I found." Lena pulled out a tube of ointment.

Britta quickly examined the packaging. "But this is for people."

"So what? We use it on Baloo, too, when he hurts himself." Lena screwed off the cap and allowed the black horse to sniff at it. "If you feed him, then I'm sure he'll stay still while I smear on the ointment."

Britta pulled a wonderfully fragrant carrot out of her pocket and held it out for the stallion on her flat hand. At the riding school, Lena had shown her the right way to do this, because the horses were always so crazy for treats that they'd have half your hand in their mouths if you didn't pay attention. But this horse was completely different. He took the carrot from her so carefully that his soft lips barely even touched Britta's hand. *Perfect*, thought Lena with satisfaction. *When Britta understands how gentle he is, she'll have no reason to be afraid anymore!* With careful movements, she applied the ointment to his black coat. Sometimes he twitched under her touch, but the horse seemed to understand that she wanted to help him and continued to hold still for her.

"Oh my, his mane and tail are partially singed."

"Bad?"

"No, I just hope that we used enough ointment," Lena mumbled with concern as she put the now empty tube back in her pocket. "Or else we'll have to take him to a veterinarian."

Britta had lost some of her timidity and fed the rest of the carrots to the horse in bite-sized pieces. Meanwhile Lena was trying, unsuccessfully, to convince Baloo that the black horse was harmless.

"Come here, my little Baloo, you have to at least sniff him!"

The dog steadfastly refused to get any closer than six feet away from the horse. He didn't even dare look straight at him. *If I even look at him, he'll eat me up*, was the expression in his sad dog eyes and Lena had to laugh. She went over to her dog and scratched his head. Then she took his head in both her hands and forced him to look at the horse.

"Take a look ... He's a vegetarian. He eats grass. You don't have to be afraid!"

Baloo struggled to free his head and then looked in the other direction, as if he had suddenly seen something very interesting over there.

"You coward. I'm no grass eater – you should be more afraid of me."

At that moment, the horse scratched the ground with his hoof because Britta didn't have any more carrots for him. That was too much for Baloo. He broke free and disappeared behind the trees.

"Well, at least he'll leave him alone." Lena stood up and went back to Britta and the horse.

"He still reeks of smoke," observed Britta, wrinkling her nose.

"Speaking of the fire, I read the entire newspaper this afternoon. There was nothing in there about a fire."

"Hmmm," mused Britta. "I didn't see any reference to one on the Internet either. I guess we'll have to hang flyers."

"You mean like what we did when we found the stray cat?"

"Yes, exactly! We could hang them all over the place – in stables and at the riding school. The horse couldn't have traveled too far last night. We'll take a picture of him and then write on our signs, 'Stray horse found!'"

"Good grief, do you have any idea how many stables there are in this area? We'll be at it for months!"

"Oh, it's not going to be that hard. After all, he's a stallion."

Lena looked at her uncomprehendingly. "So what are you saying?"

"Come on, you're the expert! Think about it; they wouldn't keep a stallion in a riding school or a riding stable – that would be too complicated if there were mares there, too. So that means that he came from a breeding stable or a private farm. And there probably aren't all that many of those around."

"I see," Lena nodded. "So what you mean is that it'll be easier to figure out where he belongs because he isn't a gelding, because he's – something more exotic?"

"Exactly! A stallion is conspicuous!"

"And you're sure – I mean, totally sure – that's he's a stallion?"

Britta snorted with laughter. "My goodness! Take a look yourself – it's impossible to overlook!"

Lena turned red and smiled. "All right, all right already. Then we'll start making signs. We can hardly take him to the lost and found office."

Meanwhile, the horse had discovered the apples in Lena's jacket and nudged her gently, requesting a taste. Lena obliged, and as she breathed in his apple breath she imagined what it would be like to own a horse like this and be able to feed it and care for it every day. What if she put an incorrect telephone number on the flyers? *But we can't just keep him*, she thought suddenly. *He can't just stay on this meadow all winter long*. Still, her mood sank when she noticed that Britta had already taken her cell phone out of her pocket to take pictures of the stallion.

"We need a name for our foundling," sighed Lena.

"Why?"

"Do you want to keep calling him 'horse'?"

"No. Shadow!"

"Huh? Where did you get that?"

"You already gave him that name yesterday, don't you remember?"

"Oh yeah," Lena grinned contritely. "Moonlight Shadow. I have to say that the name suits him, as if it were made just for him!"

Baloo waited from a safe distance until Lena was finished with her elaborate farewell to the horse. Then he ran up to her, tail wagging, and jumped up on her. He seemed to be beside himself with joy that she had managed to survive the encounter with the dangerous-looking animal. At the gate Lena pulled the old bicycle lock out of the pocket of the Icelandic sweater she always wore instead of a jacket. She carefully locked the chain.

"Do you know the combination?" asked Britta jokingly.

"That's not necessary. That's what the hedge shears are for!"

Night had fallen and a magnificent starry sky twinkled over the clearing in the woods. The stallion stood at the edge of the clearing and grazed on dark green clover.

He loved his new life. His coat felt really good and the taste of the sweet carrots and apples lingered on his tongue.

But the best part of all was the freedom.

The stallion raised his head and looked at the moon, so big and nearly full, shining down over the treetops. A shudder ran through his body. As if the moon had given him a secret command, the stallion reared up and then galloped off, kicking wildly, bucking and playing. He couldn't get enough of it – he could finally run as much as he wanted to!

Later, he stood quietly under the brilliant moon that watched over him as he slept. It was a dreamless sleep because, for the stallion, all his dreams had been fulfilled.

Chapter 5

In the early hours of the morning, a light mist rose from the meadow and heralded a radiantly clear day. The air was so cold that Lena could see her own breath as it floated away from her before it dissipated into nothing.

Baloo did not leave her side as soon as it became clear to him where they were going. Lena wore her riding breeches, because after paying a visit to Shadow she planned to go straight to her lesson. As it was every Saturday, a wonderful trail ride was scheduled. Not a single noise came from the bedrooms upstairs, so Lena quietly turned the doorknob and opened the door just wide enough for her and Baloo to slip out.

Britta was already waiting at the birch tree, hopping in place, her jacket wrapped tightly around her shivering body.

"You're certainly lively this morning!" Lena gave

her friend a playful nudge. "Aren't your calf muscles aching?"

Britta skipped more than she walked. "I'm not lively, I'm frozen half to death! And no, my legs aren't aching. We didn't bike very far at all."

"According to my tachometer, we covered more than six miles. You call that not far?"

Britta giggled. "Oh, come on. Besides, now we're familiar with all of the horse farms in the area."

Lena sighed quietly. "Yes and now there are signs everywhere with Shadow's picture, saying 'Stray horse found!' I'm sure his owner will contact us soon, and then we'll have to say goodbye to him."

"Well, for as long as we have to wait," Britta added in her jittering voice, "we should turn that shed into a cozy shelter for him. So he doesn't freeze on chilly nights."

A cold wind blew their hair in their faces when they reached the woodland garden. Britta opened the gate and lured Baloo in with a stick – the dog was still fearful of the strange black giant. Lena couldn't imagine why, especially since he wasn't the least bit shy around the riding school horses. *I hope he'll become more trusting*, she thought to herself, *or else I won't be able to take him along any more.*

Shadow raised his head in surprise when they reached the clearing, as though he hadn't expected them so early in the day. Still, he snorted and then leisurely walked over to them in order to claim his daily treats. Britta couldn't believe her eyes as Lena pulled a brittle, ancient-looking bridle out of her backpack.

"What is *that* supposed to be?"

"That, my dear Britta, is what we call a bridle," joked Lena good-naturedly.

"Very funny," grumbled Britta as she examined the old thing. "I recognize it, since it's usually hanging on the wall of your room, right?"

"Right." Lena turned the fragrant leather around in her hands and breathed in deeply. "It originally belonged to one of my aunt's horses. You know how I like to collect all the horse accessories I can get my hands on. At any rate, I spent half the night cleaning it with saddle soap and conditioning it. It wasn't easy putting it back together the right way," she added proudly.

"And now what?" Britta wanted to know. "Do you want to ride Shadow, or something?"

Lena fed the stallion an apple and held the bridle next to his head with the other hand. "It looks like it'll fit," she murmured and grinned apologetically at Britta who was gaping at her in dismay. "Don't worry. We can't ride him without a saddle anyway."

Britta approached the black horse and got very close to him. She ran her hand over the wounds on his back to examine them. "Hey, the bald spots in his coat have already healed really well! I think that ointment did the trick."

"Really? You mean his coat grew back even though we used human medicine?" joked Lena. The stallion stretched his neck and nudged her hand as she began to scratch his forehead.

"Ha, ha. Just be glad it worked. We would never have been able to afford a vet."

Shadow followed the girls inquisitively all the way to the ramshackle wooden shed, where Britta had found the hedge shears on their first night.

The shed was a mess inside. "Yuck, I didn't see all those spider webs in the night," Britta whispered in a jittery voice.

"Or all those spiders," observed Lena and laughed as Britta ran out shrieking. She grabbed the dusty broom and shooed the eight-legged critters out.

Together they cleared out the shed, and in the back they stacked badminton racquets, gardening tools, a garden hose that had been mended, bags and containers with flower seeds, hedge shears, and all sorts of odds and ends. Lena took care of the sweeping because Britta was jittery after the discovery of several more spiders. They pulled out the boards that had served as shelves and searched the wooden walls for nails that stuck out and any other potential risks for injury. By the time the shed was finally emptied and sparkling clean, their foreheads were dripping with sweat.

Lena clapped the dust and dried leaves out of

her Icelandic sweater and surveyed their work with satisfaction.

"It looks so cozy in here, I think I'll move in myself!"

Shadow stayed near them the entire time, gnawing on tree bark and observing the bluster and action, his ears perked with curiosity. When the aroma of apples and carrots found their way to his nostrils, he trotted over and poked his head into the shed.

"Hey, what's up with him?" Lena had no idea what was wrong when the stallion backed away, snorting loudly. "Do you suppose he's afraid of spiders, too?"

"Hmm," murmured Britta. "Just imagine, he was probably trapped in a burning stable. Maybe he's now afraid of all wooden sheds!"

"Oh." Lena nodded sympathetically. "He could have told us that before!"

"I have an idea. Help me over here." Britta pulled at the door. The rotted wood was held in place with two rusty hinges that just didn't want to let loose. Lena came to her aid and together they were able to lift the door off of its hinges. The entrance to the shed yawned at them like a toothless mouth.

"Ugh," groaned Britta. She dragged the door behind the shed and covered up all the gear they had stacked back there.

"Come on, now, nothing can hurt you. You can go on in!"

Lena watched tensely as Shadow first inspected the

shed from top to bottom, then slowly placed one hoof after the other into the straw before finally going all the way inside. A moment later they heard the familiar sound of lip smacking. "You're a genius," she said to Britta. "All we need now is fresh straw and he has shelter when the nights get longer and colder!"

Her friend smiled and rolled up her jacket sleeves. She glanced at her wristwatch. "Hey Lena, aren't you forgetting something?" The satisfied smile disappeared from Britta's face and was replaced by a wrinkled forehead and a look of concern.

"No, what do you mean?" Lena asked absently as she observed the stallion that was dozing happily.

"Don't you have a riding lesson today?"

"Oh darn, it completely slipped my mind! What time is it?"

"Almost quarter to ten."

"Darn it, darn it, darn it," wailed Lena. "I've got to go right now!"

"I'll stay here with Baloo and keep Shadow company for a while." Britta stepped into the shed and stroked the black stallion's soft coat. "You can pick us up on your way back home."

Lena sheepishly bit her lip as she approached Sandra. The riding teacher was sitting on a bench and looked up at her in surprise.

"You're very late, Lena!"

"Have all the horses been given out already?" Lena was concerned.

"No, don't worry. But when you're this late you have to take what's left."

"And I definitely won't complain about it today," she promised meekly.

Sandra looked at her list and acted like she was searching for Lena's name. Then, almost as an afterthought, she said, "Boomer."

Lena's face brightened.

"Don't you dare give me a hug – and hurry up, we're heading out in a few minutes!"

At the entrance to the stable, Lena bumped into Ellie, whose face was fiery red.

"Jasper looked like a pig who'd been rolling in the mud, but finally, you can see his actual coat again." She took a deep breath and then looked over at Lena with surprise. "Hey, what's up with you? You're late to riding lessons! Did somebody die? Did something terrible happen?"

Lena had to laugh. "No, I just lost track of the time. Say, if Boomer is that dirty too, can you give me a hand quickly?"

Ellie groaned, but when she saw Boomer's muddy coat she grabbed a currycomb and body brush without another word.

Boomer fidgeted and didn't want to stay still until the bridle was finally in place. The other horses were already impatient. The wind blew their manes around in the air and whistled spooky sounds in their ears. More than one horse was spooked by a sudden swirl of leaves, so that the girls sitting on their backs had their hands full trying to keep them calm. Lena mounted her horse quickly and put her feet in the stirrups.

Sandra rode across the courtyard on Misty, her gray-white mare, and drew admiring glances as always. All the riding students were envious of her excellent horsemanship and her beautiful mare that perked her delicate ears and looked about curiously as though she couldn't fathom why the other horses were so wound up. Lena had seen Misty ridden by other riders who found the mare to be erratic and overly nervous, but with Sandra's calm guidance the horse was unusually serene. Lena knew that this wasn't magic; it was genuine horsemanship.

Boomer was startled by the sound of a broom blown over by the wind and he jumped. Lena stroked his neck to comfort him and then quickly took up the reins. This was going to be quite a trail ride!

Sandra cued Misty and walked with her to the front of the group. "We're off, girls! Don't forget: always ride in single file, no passing each other and pay attention to my hand signals!"

Ellie fell in behind Lena.

"Have you heard? Over at the city stable, the roof of the covered riding arena collapsed."

"What? Did anyone get hurt?"

"No, fortunately it happed at night. But that's pretty gruesome, don't you think? Just imagine, there you are, riding in the arena without a care in the world and then suddenly the roof collapses on your head!"

Julia, who was riding in front of Boomer, turned around in her saddle. "That's not what happened. A few beams came crashing down, not the entire roof. They're repairing everything to keep the roof from actually collapsing."

"So what?" Ellie called angrily from behind. "The beams could kill you too, if they fell on your head."

Suddenly, a thought occurred to Lena that was so sinister that a cold shiver ran down her spine. "That roof…I mean, did it have anything to do with a fire?"

"You mean arson?" Ellie shook her head. "I didn't hear about anything like that. As far as I know, those beams were old and brittle."

"Why would anyone set the riding arena on fire?" Julia sneered. "If someone wanted to cause real damage, they'd set the whole stable on fire."

"But no one did that, did they?"

Ellie looked at her curiously. "What makes you think that?"

"Oh I don't know. But I read something…" Lena bit her lip. She didn't want to tell Ellie about Shadow as long as Julia was within earshot. She frantically tried to think of a way to change the subject and acted like she was busy with Boomer, who held his head up high and skeptically inspected the trees. They were swaying in the wind and making ominous creaking noises.

Sandra left the woods and turned onto a dirt path. Then she turned around in her saddle and whistled once through her teeth to call the chatty girls to attention. "We're going to trot a bit now! Pay attention. I'll take the path through the airfield. As soon as everyone is around the bend we'll start to gallop!"

Lena took up her reins and held Boomer back until the horse in front was several lengths ahead of her. Then she gave a light squeeze with her legs and guided her horse to fall into step, trotting with the others.

They weren't allowed to gallop through the airfield, but the horses knew exactly what would happen when they rounded the bend. Some of them were so excited that by the middle of the field it was hard to hold them back.

Lena had her hands full, but with steady cues she led Boomer with the reins and caught every second beat with her weight. Around the area of her tummy she felt a pleasant tingling. Then they were out of the bend. Boomer tensed all of his muscles and Lena freed his head. What an incredible feeling of flying! Lena wished that this trail and the galloping would never end! All of her thoughts of stray horses and fires in stables disappeared. Only she and Boomer existed in this wonderful moment.

Chapter 6

"Has anyone contacted you yet?" Britta's voice was just a whisper, but Mr. Anderson, their biology teacher, had ears everywhere.

"Miss Bergman, Miss Sutherland – the no-talking-during-class rule applies to you two, as well."

Lena waited until Mr. Anderson turned back to the blackboard, then shrugged her shoulders and mouthed the words, "I hope not."

An autumn storm raged outside, and their school day seemed to last forever. Lena was pleased that they had finished fixing up the shed for Shadow so that the stallion wouldn't have to stand outside in the wind and rain. *If we only had a saddle*, she thought, and drew a picture of a galloping horse in her notebook that looked a lot like Shadow. How she yearned to ride him!

"Put your notes away," Mr. Anderson commanded.

The pupils responded with a collective groan. "I'm giving you a pop quiz on genetics. I hope you've been studying and paying attention in class today."

"Oh no," Lena said anxiously. "I haven't looked at a thing!"

"It won't be that bad," Britta consoled her. "The topic is pretty easy."

"Not when you're close to getting a D like I am," Lena moaned. "This is going to be trouble."

Lena's mood had sunk to its lowest point by the time they reached the ramshackle old farm. With their pants dripping wet, they leaned their bikes against the side of the house.

"He's probably in the hay barn," Britta guessed and walked ahead. Although she had gotten as wet as Lena, it didn't bother her.

"Off we go," grumbled Lena and stomped along behind her.

The old farmer supplied the entire village with hay and straw that he harvested himself every summer. Britta knew the friendly man because she always came here to buy feed for her guinea pig– the only animal that her mother had ever allowed near her.

"Hello? Is anybody home?"

Lena looked around the barn. Very little sunlight penetrated its recesses. Spider webs hung from the rafters and bales of hay were stacked up to the top of the ceiling. When they heard a rustling sound followed by a leaping tabby cat with a mouse in her mouth, Lena almost turned on her heels to flee into the rain.

"Where could he be?" Britta mumbled. She tiptoed around the barn and then peeked through a door that was slightly ajar. Excitedly she motioned for Lena to come over to her.

"What's in there?" Lena crowded in next to her friend to peek through the door. In the weak light they saw shelves filled with dusty trophies and ribbons and walls covered with black and white photographs of jumping horses sailing over high obstacles. There was even a dusty saddle hanging on the wall.

"Are you looking for me?"

The girls whipped around. The old farmer stood in the doorway, his hands on his hips.

"We … sorry, yes, we were looking for you." Britta smiled contritely. "You see, we need straw. And hay. Two bales…how much does that cost?"

"Why do you two need so much horse feed, hmm?" The old farmer wrinkled his forehead, but his eyes sparkled merrily.

"It's supposed to be a present," Lena stated quickly. And that's not even a lie, they thought to themselves. A present for Shadow.

"Okay, let me see…let's make it five bucks; that should buy an old man a cup of coffee or two."

Britta sighed with relief and pulled the money out of her pocket. As the farmer loaded the bales into a wagon, Lena caught herself peeking again and again into the little room next to the hay storage. The trophy collection had a magnetic effect on her.

"Did you used to ride?" Lena burst out with the question when he had returned with the hay.

"Oh yes, jumping!" A dreamy expression briefly crossed his face. "We were really successful, too. It only works if you have the right horse, though. If a horse doesn't have any fun jumping, then you can just forget it. You'll never win."

"You even kept your saddle," observed Britta with admiration.

"Oh, that old thing." The farmer lifted the saddle off its hook and dropped it down on a bale of hay. The dust cloud that kicked up made Britta sneeze. "That was once a really expensive English jumping saddle," sighed the farmer, "but now it's just old and dusty. Just like me."

"The saddle is beautiful," whispered Lena. "If it were mine, I would never get rid of it either."

"Lena, come on, we have to get going." Britta glanced nervously at her watch. "Considering how muddy the ground is, we'll probably need twice as long to get where we're going."

The farmer helped them get the straw and hay bales onto their rear bicycle racks and tie them down. They

couldn't ride their bikes anymore, but they could push
them back to the garden in the woods.

"Just a minute." The farmer disappeared back into his
barn and returned with the old saddle.

"Oh my gosh …" mumbled Lena, her eyes round.

"I'd like to give this to you," said the farmer. "As long
as you promise to take good care of it!"

"We couldn't possibly accept such a gift," Britta shook
her head energetically. "No way."

"What's an old man supposed to do with a saddle that
just brings back painful memories?" The farmer smiled a
toothless grin. "If you like it, then you can keep it."

Lena held the saddle on the handlebars with one
hand as they pushed their bikes off the farm. She hardly
noticed the rain any more and her grouchy mood had
been washed away. The skin on the palm that was resting
on the old saddle tingled, as if she were holding on to a
very special secret.

Shadow stood in the middle of the clearing and grazed in
the dim light of the cloudy afternoon sky. He raised his
head, perked his ears and looked over at Lena and Britta,
but he was in no rush to walk over to them. However,
this time the girls looked especially magical; they were
pushing vehicles with huge, delicious-smelling sacks
lashed to them. They also had one of those things he
used to have buckled on his back a lot. Memories passed

through his head: a course filled with colorful obstacles and himself galloping through the middle of it.

He strolled leisurely over to the girls. They were as delighted as always when he came over to them, and they immediately pulled red apples out of their backpacks. Then they stroked and scratched him and he relished the unexpected affection. What kind of Elysian Fields had he landed in?

The girl with the braid pulled a big sack off of her vehicle and dragged it over to the shed that served as his shelter. Out of the corner of his eye, he saw the brown wolf between the trees, but was glad that the wolf still had a good deal of respect for him. The stallion sensed that the wolf did not pose a danger to him, although his instinct set off alarm bells every time he saw him and his ears lay back flat. He stood still behind the girls and watched as they grabbed fresh straw out of the sack and strewed it on the shed floor to make a soft bed for him. The simple wooden shed was nothing compared to the warm, safe stable in which the stallion had lived before all this. And his coat was not robust enough to allow him to stand outside in the cold nights. Still, the stallion knew exactly what he needed to do to keep from getting sick. He slept during the day when the sun warmed his coat. He used the cold nights to still his desire for exercise – he walked, trotted and raced around the clearing in the woods until his limbs were warm and his breath steamy in the silvery light of the moon.

As for the shelter, he would only go in there in order to eat the hay – he needed the nourishment because in the autumn the grass was short and didn't have enough nutrients. He greatly preferred to stand where he was protected by tree branches and could feel the endless expanse of the sky above him. It made him feel free and alive when his whinny resounded through the woods at night. Besides, small, claustrophobic wooden structures had stirred a feeling of dread within him ever since his escape…

The girls layered in his hay and then walked back to the clearing. Shadow followed them and watched how the girl with the braid took the leather thing and held it under his nose hopefully.

"Take a look. This is a saddle. Have you ever worn something like this on your back before?"

Shadow pushed his nose along the worn leather, inspecting it, and then snorted loudly when the smell of a strange horse got into his nostrils. Lena giggled and quickly wiped the seat with her sleeve.

"Alright then, I guess I can't impress you with this. But what do you say we give it a try?"

Lena slipped off her Icelandic sweater and carefully laid it on Shadow's back. The stallion stood as still as a statue.

"It seems as if someone here has been trained very

well," murmured Britta with surprise. She helped Lena set the saddle on the provisional saddle blanket, then took a step back and admired her handiwork. "Our saddle looks great on you," she announced with satisfaction.

Meanwhile, Lena had gone back to the shed and returned with the old bridle. Shadow looked like a real pro. He freely took the bit in his mouth and even lowered his head so that Lena didn't have to stand on tiptoes to reach his neck. "Three fingers under the throat lash, two fingers under the noseband," Lena spoke out loud to help her remember all the rules of bridling. What a strange feeling! Up until now, Sandra had checked all her preparatory work. This was the first time that it was all her responsibility alone. *Hopefully I'm doing everything right*, she thought to herself nervously, feeling extremely grateful to have Britta there with her.

"Do you want to go first or should I?" Lena looked at her friend, her eyes sparkling.

"You," Britta decided quickly.

Shadow perked his ears in anticipation as Lena led him on the line to the middle of the meadow. "You'd probably rather go outside to really stretch your legs, huh? But for today, we'd better stay in here. If all goes well, then we'll ride through the woods together – promise!"

Lena pulled the girth tight and adjusted the stirrups. The stallion didn't move an inch and Lena noticed that her heart, which had been pounding quickly, had gradually returned to normal. She took the reins in one hand, pushed off from the ground and swung her leg over the horse's back. *Whew*, she thought, *it's a good thing I'm used to Katja, because she's even taller than Shadow!*

Shadow lowered his head and began to chew on the bridle bit. Lena quickly reached forward and stroked his deep black neck. "Relax, handsome! Come on, we'll go for a little walk." She took the reins in both hands and gently and carefully squeezed his belly with her legs, the way she had learned to do it with Boomer. Shadow threw up his head and marched off. It all went so fast that Lena had a hard time taking up the reins quickly enough.

"Slow down, Shadow, wooooah!" Lena tugged on the reins and attempted to lead the stallion to a slower gait, but Shadow just went faster and faster until he was practically trotting. *Oh my gosh*, Lena thought with fright. *I can't stop him*. She tugged and pulled on the reins and felt her entire body stiffen with panic. Fearful thoughts raced through her head as Shadow continued to accelerate with each stride.

Then a brilliant idea struck her. All of a sudden, it was as if Sandra were walking alongside of her, calling out directions to her the way she did the first time Lena rode Boomer. *Boomer isn't as worn in and desensitized as the other school horses, Lena, so you'll have to be very careful with his reins. Never pull back hard; give signals gently. And don't sit so stiffly in the saddle; stay nice and loose! Otherwise the horse will run right out from under you.*

Although it seemed crazy to loosen up on the reins of a trotting horse, Lena followed Sandra's directions. She took the pressure off the stallion's mouth and soon noticed that the horse was calming down. Slowly her muscles relaxed, too, and she sat up in the saddle and tried hard to maintain correct posture, with her back straight and her heels down.

After just one more round, Shadow chomped on the bit and walked at a calmer pace. Lena changed to the other hand and attempted to let the stallion trot. Again, she squeezed his belly as gently as possible with her legs, and once again, Shadow shot forward. But this time, Lena didn't pull back on the reins frantically – she sat calmly in the saddle. This had worked well when Shadow was walking. Now that he was trotting it seemed to work even better. Shadow chomped on the bit and carried Lena so many times around the clearing and with such a bounce in his stride that his rider was completely out of breath when she slowed the stallion down to a stop in the middle of the clearing. Overjoyed, she stroked and patted his neck before she glided down from the saddle.

"Britta, that was incredible –"

A thunderclap in the distance caused Shadow to quickly raise his head, and the sound of a dog barking came from between the trees. Lena noticed with alarm that the sky had darkened not only as a result of the storm clouds blowing in, but also because it was quite late in the afternoon. When she was riding Shadow, she had completely lost track of the time!

Britta smiled a little lopsidedly. "Time out," she called. "Let's ride home fast."

Working rapidly, they slipped the bridle over the stallion's head and unbuckled the saddle from his back. They stored both in the shed, high up on an overhead beam. Lena felt guilty because the weather was being so unfair to Britta.

Baloo waited next to the bicycles and whimpered at the sky while Lena quickly thanked Shadow for the ride with an apple. "Be just as nice tomorrow when Britta rides you," she asked him quietly before planting a kiss on the velvety horse nose. "Good bye, Shadow – see you tomorrow!"

The sky darkened rapidly after the girls locked the gate and pushed their bikes up the dirt path. Not a single twinkling star was to be seen; even the moon was covered by the incoming storm clouds. When they reached the wide woodland trail, both girls winced when they saw the first flashes of lightning over the treetops. Lena pedaled furiously, although she had to watch herself constantly to avoid running over Baloo, who was running wildly with her. When they reached the edge of the woods, a sinister wall of dark clouds heralded a violent thunderstorm.

Plump, cold raindrops soaked Lena's Icelandic sweater as she opened the garage door. She was happy to be out of the storm. Unfortunately, the minute she opened the door she realized that some thunder and lightning had been waiting for her at home in the form of her father, who walked out of the kitchen and looked at her, his arms crossed across his chest.

"Where are you coming from so late?"

"Oh, hi Dad. I, uh, was with Baloo."

"Lena, listen to me. Your mother told me that it's been like this all week. You can't keep disappearing all day long and wandering around with Britta or Baloo and completely ignoring your homework. Your teacher called us – he's concerned about you, says that you are unable to concentrate and poorly prepared for class." Mr. Bergman had a serious expression on his face. "Lena, tell me what's wrong. Are you having problems?"

Lena bit her lip. Should she tell her father about Shadow? But what would Britta say if she just blabbed their secret before her friend had her chance to ride Shadow? That wouldn't be fair, Lena decided, and shook her head silently. Once Britta had her chance to ride – then she'd tell him.

"Alright then," sighed Mr. Bergman. "Maybe it was just a one time slip-up. The next time you come home with a bad grade, however, you'll be grounded."

Chapter 7

"Britta, would you like to help me set up a jumping course?"

Sandra lifted her nose out of the notebook and began to laugh when she saw the surprised faces of her riding students.

"What do you mean – set up a course?"

"Are we jumping today? Really? The entire lesson?"

"Oh, cool! Can I have Jasper? Please, Sandra, please?"

Lena excitedly shifted her weight from one leg to the other. Jumping was her great passion. Now there was only one more thing she needed to be happy – Boomer!

"Okay, as you may have heard, the riding school in the city had a problem with its covered riding arena. They have had to completely re-do their entire roof and the work is taking longer than they had expected. Unfortunately, the big fall jumping tournament is in two weeks and they asked us if we could host it here."

Ellie fidgeted around with excitement. "Does that mean we all get to participate?"

"All of you can start in the novice level, yes. It's just a small event, but it will draw more than a hundred participants from the entire region! That's why this week and next we'll be practicing intensely, so that our riding club doesn't embarrass itself!" Sandra winked but Lena was quite certain that Sandra was serious about not wanting to be embarrassed.

"Okay girls, let's get to the horses. Each of you should choose a horse that you feel comfortable with and that feels comfortable with you. Ellie?"

Ellie chose Jasper, the jokester. He was her favorite horse and no one had a problem with that. Each of the other riding students had a favorite horse and the process of assigning the horses continued without an argument. At the end, two horses were left: Katja, the placid old mare and Boomer, the young gelding. Lena looked at Julia from the corner of her eyes. The other girl wasn't about to give up without a fight and leave Boomer to her.

"Now we'll get to you two. I don't even need to ask which horse you'd like to ride in the tournament. Could you two peacefully work out which of you will get Boomer?"

Julia cleared her throat clumsily. "Well, since I just rode Boomer in our last dressage lesson with the new running reins, I think it would be best for him not to be confused by another rider. I'll ride him."

"You can forget that," Lena called out angrily. "I ride him just as well as you do and I love him! You only want him because you can't win with Katja!"

"Oh yeah? Who couldn't even get Katja to canter last time? I've never had a problem with her." Julia ran her hand through her hair and two of her friends murmured their agreement.

"Then why don't you ride her, if you're so good at it," Lena hissed back at her.

Sandra sighed. She picked two straws of hay from the ground, and ripped one in half. She covered both straws with her fingers and held them up to the girls. "Alright then, we'll be fair about it: whoever draws the shorter straw will ride Katja."

Julia wasted no time and drew the right straw. A satisfied smile spread across her face as she held her straw next to Lena's. "I hope Katja doesn't fall asleep on the course; that would be embarrassing for our club," she called over her shoulder before disappearing into Boomer's box.

Lena was close to tears. "She saw it; she knew which one was the longer straw."

"Lena, that's not true. And now that's the end of the discussion – you two can be grateful that I'm even letting you participate in the tournament." With that, Sandra turned on her heel and disappeared in the direction of the covered riding arena.

"Try not to take it so hard," Britta tried to comfort her. "Besides, Katja is the more experienced horse. Maybe she'll jump even better than Boomer in the tournament."

Lena made a face. "I don't care about winning – I just want to ride Boomer, that's all. But she's always trying to get between Boomer and me. If only he belonged to me!"

Britta shrugged her shoulders and quickly ran off after Sandra to help her out. Lena felt bad almost immediately. She knew Britta would have liked to ride, too, she thought dejectedly. And it wouldn't have made any difference to her which horse she got, as long as she was allowed to ride.

While she was being groomed, Katja stood the entire time with her head hanging, as if she, too, were resigned to her fate. She seemed to be tired of all the riding students who came day in and day out and pulled and tugged her along. Poor Katja, thought Lena suddenly, nobody really liked her. No wonder she was so listless. Maybe Britta was right. Boomer was young and inexperienced, while Katja had participated in plenty of tournaments in her life. What if she really did jump better than the young gelding? *Julia took Boomer away from me*, Lena thought darkly. *Just for that, I'll beat her in the tournament.*

Jasper was having one of his silly days, acting as if he had never seen an obstacle before and taking a wide detour around the colorful poles, which wasn't particularly easy in the small covered riding arena. Ellie cracked up every time he threw his head and snorted at the obstacles, as if goblins were sitting on top of them.

"Ellie, do you think you'll be able to make it over a single obstacle today or should I just cross you off the list of participants right now?" Sandra was tired of the gelding's tricks.

"He's behaving like a foal," gasped Ellie, but when she saw the expression on Sandra's face, she took up the reins and gave Jasper a light tap with the crop. "That's enough now, or we won't be in the tournament!"

Lena thought it was hilarious to observe Jasper's face as the joker in him suddenly disappeared. It was as if someone had flipped a switch; suddenly he was jumping obediently over all the obstacles, not making a single fault. Ellie couldn't believe her luck.

"Very nice. And at the tournament, just make sure you leave out the comedy show in the beginning. Julia is up next!"

Lena maneuvered into a corner to keep from getting in the way and squinted to watch Boomer. The gelding was nervous. He had never jumped over so many obstacles in a row. But he could – and how! With a powerful push off, he flew over the poles and cleared them with room to spare, as if the height were just child's play for him. Shortly before the last obstacle, it happened; Boomer landed and shot out of the curve with such momentum that he passed the last obstacle before Julia could react.

"Very good jumping," Sandra praised her, "but in the tournament, you would have been disqualified on that last jump. Try to ride him more calmly. The obstacles aren't high; he can take them in his sleep. Faults on a course are always the rider's fault. Lena is up."

"Now show them what you can do, girl!" Lena rode into the middle and cued Katja with a forceful squeeze with her legs into a clunky trot. She had to think about the day before when she rode Shadow in the clearing. What a difference compared to lazy old Katja! They galloped on the closed side of the ring and approached the first obstacle, a simple vertical. Katja slowed a little, but then jumped anyway and Lena was heaved forward with a strong jolt. She quickly straightened herself in the saddle and urged Katja out of the swinging trot she had fallen back into. The next obstacle, an oxer, went far more smoothly, but it took all of Lena's energy to keep Katja at canter. They made it over the wall without a fault, and then took the combination and the last vertical, where the top pole was higher than the other obstacles. Lena allowed Katja to slow down to a slow walk and looked over at Sandra expectantly.

"Not bad, Lena, but you *ride* too little. Don't let Katja decide for herself when she should set off. *You* need to determine when to jump. When the jumps are higher it's especially important to go with the movements of your horse. Aside from that, it was a good fault-free ride. Just work on getting Katja to gallop more evenly."

Sandra let all of them jump the course one more time, then she clapped her hands and, for the first time that day, wore a look of satisfaction on her face. "Very good girls, I'm proud of you! That was quite an achievement for each of you. Now go ahead and ride the horses dry. We'll practice again next week."

"It worked out well with Katja after all," said Ellie as she let the chestnut mare catch up.

"Yes," Lena admitted. "But with Boomer, it would have been a hundred times more fun."

With squealing tires, the big SUV came to a stop next the massive chestnut tree. The ground shook as a heavy-set man jumped out of the car and slammed the door loudly. Rain poured off the roof and dripped mercilessly down his neck. He angrily folded up the collar of his black leather jacket.

With large strides he hurried around the car and squinted to read the flyer that was pinned to the tree, waving in the wind. He recognized the horse in the picture – but what was it doing still alive?

"Stray horse," the man murmured. Could it be possible?

Nervously, he ran a hand over his bald head and felt

himself break out in a sweat despite the rain. It couldn't be. That one deal brought him as much money as he earned working hard in the stable all year long – he wasn't about to risk losing all that!

He gave the horse in the photograph an evil look, tore the sign from the tree and shoved it into his jacket pocket. A cold wet wind blew at his back as he got into his SUV and raced off. The wheels in his head were already churning furiously.

A light wind blew the clouds and tousled Lena's hair as she unlocked the gate to the woodland garden. Britta had been quiet the entire time and Lena struggled with her guilty conscience for whining so much over how the horses were divided up.

"Oh Britta, I'm sorry. I didn't mean to carry on like that about Katja."

Britta smiled and stretched her hands toward Shadow, who was approaching them from the trees with his ears perked at them. She took his head in her arms and laid her cheek on his forehead.

"That's okay," she said lightly, but her eyes looked absently at the cloudy sky. What was wrong with her?

Lena decided that the stallion should be all Britta's today day. "Wait with him. I'll get the saddle and bridle and then you can ride him for as long as you want, okay?"

Britta had thoroughly groomed his dark coat by the time Lena returned with the saddle. Together they saddled and bridled the stallion. Again, he held perfectly still, as if he were glued to the spot.

"Just imagine how crazy things would get if we didn't tie up our riding school horses when we saddled them," laughed Lena.

"That's another reason why it makes no sense that no one's missing him," said Britta coolly. "Such a strikingly beautiful black horse, that's well-trained on top of that! But no one has reacted to our posters."

"Lucky for us, or can you imagine giving him up again?" Lena giggled, but Britta looked genuinely worried. "If only we knew what happened to him."

Lena tightened the girth and led the stallion to the middle of the clearing, just as she had the day before. She held out the stirrups for her friend. "Here, I'll hold him for you until you're up in the saddle."

Britta pulled her hands into her sleeves and chewed nervously on her lower lip.

"Well, you know, I think I'd rather watch a little more before I ride him myself."

Surprised, Lena mounted him herself and allowed the stallion to start off, calmly, without tugging at the reins.

This time Shadow didn't dash off, but instead lowered his head and began to chomp on the bit as soon as Lena gently took up the reins.

"That looks really professional," Britta enthusiastically praised her.

Lena took the reins up a little bit more and let the stallion start trotting. She tried a few school figures, which wasn't all that easy in the round clearing. On the far side she had to sidestep a fallen pine tree that stretched into the clearing and blocked the way. She used the unwieldy obstacle to ride around it in serpentines and happily concluded that Shadow was even better than Boomer at responding to the most gentle leg cues.

"Wow, he moves so well," she called out enthusiastically in the middle of the clearing. "Do you mind if I try to canter with him before you ride?"

"Go ahead," Britta answered generously. "I can't do more than walk with him anyway."

Today everything worked perfectly with him, Lena thought to herself cockily, and she gave the canter cues that she had learned. Shadow seemed to have been waiting for them. He gave a little leap of joy, shook his head enthusiastically and shot off. *Yowza*, thought Lena, *the same game as yesterday; now just don't tug at the reins*. At the crazy speed they were going, she found it incredibly difficult to sit calmly in the saddle and give the next commands. She concentrated, and alternately took up the reins and loosened them until she felt that the stallion was actually calming down and responding to the reins. *I can do it*, Lena cheered to herself, *I can really ride him!*

With all her attention directed toward slowing down, Lena forgot to steer. When she realized that they were heading toward a fallen tree at full speed, it was too late. A scream rang out and at that moment Lena didn't know if it came from her, or from Britta. In her fright, she just managed to gasp for air when the stallion leaped and sailed over the tree.

Afterwards Lena could not explain how she had managed to stay in the saddle. Her heart pounded furiously, but she managed to slow Shadow to a trot and then a walk without falling off. Shadow snorted and puffed and Lena had the feeling that he wanted nothing more than to have another go at that obstacle.

"Lena, oh my goodness, Lena, are you okay? What were you doing out there? You could have broken your neck!"

Lena patted Shadow's black neck absently and glided down from the saddle. She could hardly believe what had just happened out there! Her knees were wobbly and she had to lean against the stallion to keep from toppling over, but when she looked into Britta's wide-open eyes, she almost laughed out loud.

"Did you see that? What a crazy horse!"

"*You're* the one who's crazy! Why did you do that? The tree is nearly as high as Shadow!"

"I didn't do it on purpose. Shadow kept getting faster and faster. I was trying to slow him down, and by the time I noticed that he was heading straight for the obstacle, it was too late. I couldn't do anything, so I just held tight and – yes." Now she really did have to laugh. Out of relief. She shook her head as she gauged the tree's height.

"Hey," she said cockily. "He sure can jump – maybe I should participate in the tournament with Shadow instead? Julia sure would take notice."

Britta's face was still chalk-white from fright. "Lena, I'm just thankful that you're still alive and you're already making dumb jokes."

"It wasn't *that* bad. Fortunately Sandra taught us how to jump with a horse; otherwise I would probably have gone flying. But I instinctively did the right thing: sat loosely, didn't distract the horse in his mouth and went with the movement." She grabbed the stirrup and held it for her friend. "So, now you finally get your turn."

Britta stumbled backwards as though she were afraid the saddle might bite her. "Uh, no, I think we should postpone it."

"Are you afraid or something?" Lena couldn't believe it. "That's why you didn't want to ride before – right?"

"You know, on a riding school horse it's completely different. But out here…well, I just saw what can happen."

95

"I'll walk alongside the entire time and lead him with the reins. Don't be afraid, it's such an incredible feeling to ride him."

But Britta sadly shook her head. "Let's just go move that tree instead, okay?"

Chapter 8

The trail to the woodland garden was so familiar to them by now that it felt as if they had been walking that way all their lives. Every tree, every low hanging branch, seemed to have become a party to their secret and Lena desperately wished that the autumn would lead straight to a blooming spring instead of the cold, frosty winter that made Shadow's future so uncertain. The rusty old chain hung like a symbol of the past over a rotted post near the entrance and Lena thought back with amusement to the time when she would count the links and draw pictures in order to see if anyone ever went in or out of the garden. *At least we know the answer to that now*, she thought to herself.

Shadow stood under a group of pine trees and looked out at the clearing, like a sailor looking out at the ocean. It had rained hard all night long and in the clearing the water stood in muddy puddles. Now the rain had eased into a gentle drizzle, but the ground was extra soft and soggy and Lena felt as if she was sinking in with her riding boots.

"What miserable weather," complained Britta, who was wearing sneakers and had wet socks as a result. "Wouldn't you rather go to your riding lesson instead? I'd prefer a warm, dry riding arena to this muddy puddle."

"But today is Saturday – trail ride day! Weather like this doesn't bother Sandra a bit. I'm sure she wouldn't stay inside in the arena just because of a little rain." Lena was the first to reach the cluster of trees, and she gently ran her hand over the black horse's wet neck. His coat shimmered and looked as if he had showered in shoe polish instead of rain. Lena loved the smell of wet horse that drifted into her nose. "Hello, Shadow," she whispered and gently ran her fingers through his long mane. "I've never missed a riding lesson, but today I'm doing it so that we can both ride. What do you say to that?"

The stallion snorted because a wave of raindrops landed directly on his nose; Lena interpreted it as agreeing with her question. How wonderful this horse was! "He's the kind of horse you'd like to take home, put in your closet and just gaze at all day long," was how Britta had put it recently. Lena hated the thought of having to give him up one day.

"Aren't we incredibly lucky that nobody has contacted us yet about our flyer?" Britta asked, as if she were reading Lena's mind.

"Yes," Lena agreed, absentmindedly. "But there just has to be a legal owner."

"Maybe he died in the fire that Shadow escaped from," suggested Britta, her voice so serious that Lena looked at her with a frightened expression. "Hey, that was a joke, ha, ha!"

"Do you think we should make a few more flyers?"

"I don't know. We could place an ad in the newspaper, but I'm afraid that my mother might read it. If she finds out that we've been taking care of a big black horse for weeks, she'd tear my head off."

Lena laughed. "You know what, I've decided that we're not going to ride in the clearing here today. Let's go for a trail ride in the woods where we'll be a little more protected from the rain than here on the meadow."

Britta nodded, but Lena wasn't sure if she simply hadn't heard the word "we" or if she didn't want to talk about it. Britta had to muster up the courage to ride, she thought, otherwise she would regret it later.

Britta walked off to pick up the saddle that she'd hung up over a narrow beam in the shed. Lena used the sleeve of her Icelandic sweater to wipe the worst of the dirt off Shadow's wet back, and then she stood aside to allow her friend to saddle and bridle him. She was almost jealous of how self-assured Britta's movements were. Especially since she had only learned them from books, Lena thought with amazement.

Shadow stomped impatiently with his front legs. Lena reached for the reins and led him along the path around the clearing to the entry gate. Outside she suddenly had a strangely queasy feeling. In the fenced-in garden, the adventure wasn't quite as risky, but what would they do if Shadow were to throw her and race off through the woods, with stirrups swinging? *Nonsense*, she reprimanded herself. *I didn't fall off the last time; I'll manage to stay on today, too.* With resolve she pulled herself into the saddle and cued the stallion to set off. Britta had to jog every few steps to keep up.

The treetops caught the raindrops and allowed a few cold droplets here and there to slip down Lena's collar. She had to concentrate to keep from losing control of the powerful stallion that was looking around inquisitively. He was quite boisterous, yet things like tree stumps and anthills startled him. "He sure is in a rush," wheezed Britta. When they reached a long, wide woodland trail that gently snaked up a small hill, Lena felt all of the horse's muscles tense up under her. "Britta, I'm going to let him trot up, okay? We'll meet you again on the way down!" Lena didn't even wait for her friend's answer and instead eased the pressure of her legs and just barely loosened the reins. The stallion shot off and trotted up the hill with massive strides. Lena didn't have a chance to be frightened; the fast trot simply felt wonderful!

"Did he bolt again?" Britta asked with concern when Lena was back with her. She was completely out of breath.

"No, he stopped very obediently. He just needed to have a little fun. You see? Now he's totally calm." Lena patted his black neck and took her feet out of the stirrups. "Okay, it's your turn!"

Britta protested, but Lena jumped out of the saddle and paid no attention.

"Come on, you scaredy cat. You've ridden Boomer before and he's just as wild as Shadow!"

Lena held the stallion by the reins while Britta climbed up into the saddle. No sooner was she sitting up there and allowing her hand to glide over the black neck than a pleasant smile spread over her face. Satisfied, Lena took a step back.

Britta took the reins and carefully cued the stallion to begin. With some surprise, Lena had to acknowledge that her friend was doing a fantastic job, as if she had secretly been taking riding lessons. Shadow strode calmly and confidently next to Lena and even stopped being startled by the woodland spirits and the tree stumps, as if he didn't want to make Britta any more nervous.

"Just look at what a beautiful trail this is! I think Shadow would like to trot again."

"Then you try it." Britta looked down at her with such trepidation that Lena almost had to laugh out loud.

"Oh, come on now, give it a try! I'll run next to you to make sure he doesn't try anything foolish."

"But will I be able to get him to stop again?" Britta asked nervously.

"Of course. You sit solidly in the saddle and shorten both reins at the same time."

Lena found it difficult to run in her riding boots. She had trouble keeping pace with the black horse and had to let go of his reins halfway. Her friend didn't notice until they had reached an intersection that she alone was in control of the stallion, and she slowed him down almost exactly according to the rules. With her eyes shining, she looked down to Lena.

"This is so much fun! Thank you for talking me into trying it!"

Lena grinned. "And just look at how well you get along with him – better than I do!"

"That's ridiculous. I feel like a marionette whose strings have been cut. My knees were shaking, and the whole time I was afraid that he would dash straight into the woods because he didn't understand what I wanted him to do."

Lena laughed. She boisterously patted the stallion on his neck but then suddenly he stumbled back a step in fright, tossed his head and let out a bloodcurdling whinny.

"Hey, watch my poor ears. What's eating you?"

Britta stroked his tensed neck. "He must have heard something."

Lena looked at her friend and started to giggle. "Do you know what this reminds me of?"

"Yes, but I hardly think that another half-incinerated horse is going to jump out of the woods at us. Maybe he heard a deer."

"Be quiet a minute – there really is something!" Lena listened carefully. The stallion was getting more and more impatient. He stomped with his front legs and held his head and ears high, as if it were easier to hear sounds up there. "I hear voices!"

"Hikers?"

"No, it sounds like…" Shadow let out another whinny, loud and demanding. He stomped with his hooves and tossed his head impatiently from side to side. Lena thought quickly and grabbed the reins.

Please don't let the stallion bolt!

"Come on, back to the garden, fast!"

"Easy for you to say," Britta shortened the reins and tried to lead the stallion in a particular direction. But Lena had to marshal up all her strength before the horse finally came along. She braced herself against the reins and didn't ease up, even when her fingers began to burn painfully. Again and again, Shadow tried to turn around, to raise his head and run to the unknown person.

"Let me get down," Britta begged. The hair on her neck was standing on end.

"No," gasped Lena, who was trying to keep her voice sounding calm. "You need to stay up there; it's the best way to control him. If both of us tug at his reins he'll just tear himself away and bolt, believe me."

They worked together to urge the upset horse onwards, and struggled along the muddy path. Lena was relieved when they finally reached the gate. There was hardly any time to send a prayer heavenward – *Please let the chain be unlocked* – before they opened the gate with their clammy fingers. They didn't dare to take a deep breath until Shadow and Britta were in safety, inside the fenced in garden. Britta stood on wobbly knees and held the horse by the reins while he whinnied shrilly and fidgeted around her.

"Quick, let's take off his bridle, and then he can run and blow off steam as much as he wants!" Lena gasped from all the exertion. Britta undid the girth and grabbed the saddle with both hands before the stallion shot off and disappeared behind the trees before running along the fence like a caged tiger.

"Wow, for a minute there I didn't believe that we'd make it back!" Britta leaned against a tree and looked at her friend with anxious eyes. "What in the world just happened out there?"

Lena listened a little, but the sounds had stopped. Only

the gentle rain disturbed the silence of the woods – not counting Shadow's penetrating calls.

"That was the riding class! Sandra usually prefers to ride through the airfield, except when it's raining because the ground there gets so muddy."

"Oh my gosh!" Britta raised her hand to her mouth in shock. "Then they must have heard us!"

"Not us, but Shadow." Lena sighed. Had the stallion just given away their secret? In her mind's eye, she already saw people stomping around their garden, driving up with heavy horse trailers to pick up Shadow. "Do you suppose they'll come to take a look?"

Britta shook her head, deep in thought. "They'll think that there was another rider on the trail. Why would they expect to find a horse in the middle of the woods? No. But we do have to be a lot more careful next time."

"I'm glad that it turned out okay this time!" Lena helped Britta to put away the saddle and they said goodbye to Shadow, who was still trying to peek through the thick pine trees along the fence.

"Come on, let's go. He's not interested in us anymore today. Besides, my feet are sopping wet!"

"Alright then," Lena frowned. "I suppose that means I'll have to spend the rest of the day trying to learn about genetics."

Shadow's whinnying resounded through the woods even

long after the girls had left the garden. Again and again he would stop and listen. In the twilight he waited and hoped. For an answer. An answer from the horses that had been so near to him.

He had been alone for so long that he hadn't noticed how much he missed companionship. In his old home, he only came in contact with fellow horses through the bars of his box or in the ring. Somehow he hadn't noticed that something was missing. Here it was different. He had the girls and the cowardly wolf, but that just wasn't the same.

His calls were swallowed by the night and the stallion knew that the others were gone. All of them. In his whole horse life, he had never felt as lonely as he did that night. He looked at the moon through the tops of the pine trees, as if he were searching for an answer. *What's wrong with me?* his expression seemed to ask. But the others had called back to him the same way that he called to them, curiously, inquisitively. The memory haunted him and left him wandering about, restlessly, impatiently. He was happy in his new home. Here in this garden was where he had discovered freedom. But his instinct would not leave him in peace. It mercilessly sent images of horses in big herds and mares with long-legged, clumsy foals through his thoughts. He could fight against a fire, but he couldn't fight against his very nature.

Shadow raced down to the clearing and bucked in the middle of the meadow, as though he wanted to whisper something to the moon as it rose up above the treetops. However many days and nights it would take – the other horses would come again. Then he only had to prove to them what a good protector he was, and convince them with all his energy and spirit that he was one of them and belonged with them. Then, finally, he wouldn't be alone anymore under the starry sky.

Chapter 9

"I have to show you something else!" Britta slammed her biology book closed and stretched out on Lena's bed. "Turn on you computer."

Lena obeyed. "Thanks for helping me study," she murmured. "I never would have understood it by myself."

"That's okay." Britta smiled. "Besides, you help me with riding."

Lena went online and made room for Britta in front of the screen. Her eyes got bigger and bigger with amazement as Britta uploaded a website on missing horses. There were photos, descriptions and stories about the beloved animals.

"Did you see Shadow here or something? whispered Lena.

Britta shook her head. "No."

"Well then, why are you showing it to me?"

Britta sighed and rolled her eyes. "Precisely for that reason! Lena, this is an international site for missing horses. If a horse disappears or is stolen, then the owner can upload pictures and include all sorts of information about them. And if someone finds the horse or recognizes it at a farmer's market or auction, then this is where he can go to locate the owner."

"I've read about that," said Lena with surprise. "But you said that Shadow isn't in here?"

"Nope, no Shadow." Britta clicked on a photo of a black horse. "I read through every post last night. No one seems to be missing our stray."

"Our strange black horse," murmured Lena. "He's surrounded by mystery."

"Do you know why I wanted to look for information on him?" Britta raised her eyebrows and didn't give Lena any time to answer her. "Because of his super jump. My guess is that he was a jumping horse in a past life."

Suddenly, the plan that had been going through her head all last evening, ever since that fateful phone call from Ellie, came. Lena bit her lip. "You know, Britta, I've been wanting to talk to you about that, too. There was an accident yesterday during riding lessons. You remember when we heard them in the woods? The horses went wild, and Katja wound up stumbling and she sprained her fetlock. Ellie said that it isn't serious, but Katja can't take part in the jumping tournament."

The corners of Britta's mouth twitched as she sensed what it was that her friend wanted. "And now you want to jump with Shadow, right?"

Lena followed a trail of dust under her bed. "Mm hmm, well, I thought only if it was okay with you."

Britta stood up and walked over to the window. "Lena, we don't know anything at all about Shadow. You jumped with him once and that was so dangerous!"

Lena jumped up, too. "Then let's give it another try! Oh please, Britta, if you'd help me then I know I could do it. We'll set up a few obstacles in the woods and practice with him. If it doesn't work, then I'll back out of the tournament." She looked at her friend beseechingly. "Yes?"

"You're crazy." Britta looked over at the door from which they suddenly heard the patter of a child's footsteps. "All right, then. I suppose we could give it a try. But I also think that we have to put information about Shadow online." She grinned as Lena let the corners of her mouth hang downward. "Now don't look at me like that. I didn't say we had to do it today."

Britta helped look between the trees for suitable twigs and branches that they could pile up in the clearing to make obstacles. Fortunately the rain hadn't started again and most of the puddles in the meadow had drained.

"Three jumps; that should do for a first try," said Britta, rubbing her dirty hands on her pants.

The obstacles on the meadow didn't look half as inviting as the colorful poles in the riding club and they weren't especially high, either. *But if he jumps here, then he'll do it there, too*, Lena encouraged herself. She shoved her foot into the stirrup and hopped up for momentum. Just then, Baloo shot out of the woods like a rocket and chased after a rabbit, barking loudly. Shadow gave a start and Lena struggled to keep her balance.

"Hey, dog, cut the silliness!" Baloo came to a stop in the middle of the meadow and barked with satisfaction, as if to say, *Mission accomplished – the bunny is gone*. Lena pulled herself up in the saddle, shook her head and looked down at the charcoal colored mutt as he carefully inspected each of the homemade obstacles. "Do you mind putting off your battles with assorted woodland creatures until later? This is not a good time for the horse to shy." She rode up to the obstacle, and like the rabbit he had been chasing, Baloo fled into the nearby pine trees.

"Please be careful, Lena!" Britta took her place on the path that went around the clearing and chewed her lower lip nervously. Lena gave her an encouraging smile and then forgot everything around her, concentrating instead on the powerful horse under her.

"Okay, relax. First we have to get you warmed up." She let the stallion trot, rode a few school figures, changed the lead and noticed how her own muscles loosened up with each new round. When she finally

headed for the first obstacle, Shadow seemed to float over the ground. Lena hardly felt how he took the branch with one smooth jump.

"Terrific!" she whispered toward the perked horse ears. "And now all three!"

Shadow snorted. The head wind whistled through his ears and his mane bounced in rhythm with his powerful strides. The jumps were so low that he hardly took note of the branches. He was accustomed to different obstacles, some as tall as a man holding up poles you could walk under. Still, here no one tugged on his reins, or jammed sharp spurs into his belly. He didn't feel the sharp whip, either; just the flyweight of the girl who seemed about to burst with joy. Whether it was her sense of happiness that had transferred to him or simply his newfound lust for life, Shadow didn't care. His legs jumped by themselves, and his hooves pushed off from the ground as if they never wanted to land there again.

Never in his entire life had he felt such complete joy in jumping. At this moment, he could have out-jumped any opponent.

A few steps away from Britta, Lena slowed Shadow down and came to a stop in front of her friend. Lena's eyes sparkled.

"And – what do you think? Doesn't he jump brilliantly?"

"In all honesty?" Britta stepped into the clearing with

a mysterious expression on her face. "I'd say that you're a sure thing for the championship," she finally smiled.

Lena dismounted and hugged her friend. "Thanks, Britta. You have no idea how much that means to me!"

"Hey, enough already!" Britta laughed as she freed herself. She stroked Shadow's nose. "And we're beside you if you two don't win!"

Lena watched Britta ride a few rounds in the clearing. She stood in the middle of the meadow and called out directions to her friend the way Sandra always did with her. "Heels down, Britta! Ride on the circle. Guide with your legs and not with the reins!"

Britta's face was red from exertion by the time she got down off Shadow. "That was my first official riding lesson," she called out happily.

"You really did a great job," Lena admitted, "as if you rode in a previous life."

"You know something? I think it's because I've spent so much time watching how all of you do it. And because I read so much about it."

"But I'll bet it feels a lot nicer on a real horse than in the books, right?" Lena laughed. She walked over to Shadow and patted his neck.

The stallion suddenly raised his head and perked his ears. His entire body stiffened and he let out a deep rumble. Lena followed his gaze and saw the leaves rustle. Someone had been watching them.

Lena held her breath and saw her own shock reflected in Britta's eyes. *Oh, no!* she thought. *We forgot to lock the chain!* She wanted to knock her head against a tree. Now it was all over. Suddenly a completely different thought shot through her head; Baloo! Where was he, anyway? And why hadn't he reacted?

The leaves rustled again and someone disappeared into the woods above the clearing. The figure was small and there was something strangely familiar about it. And then suddenly she knew why the dog hadn't barked – because he knew the intruder.

Britta was the first to get hold of herself again. She took a few timid steps, and then when she saw the small figure try to flee she raced after it. But Lena knew how to stop the intruder. He had to realize that he had been found out. And all that was necessary was a shout.

"Larry!"

Britta stopped dead in her tracks. The small figure now slunk out from between the pine trees. Baloo rubbed against his legs like a cat and didn't show the slightest bit of remorse.

"You little traitor," Lena scolded angrily, and at that moment she wasn't sure whether she was saying it to the dog or to her brother. She was close to tears. Larry was a little tattletale. He would run home and blab everything to their parents right down to the smallest detail. She looked at Britta helplessly. Her friend had to think of something.

115

"So, isn't that a nice horse?" Britta asked in a sweet-as-sugar voice. She put her arm around the boy and pushed him toward the stallion. Larry was reluctant; he had enormous respect for animals that were bigger than he was. Britta noticed this and quickly gave Lena a triumphant look. "Would you like to ride him?"

"No, I don't wanna!" Larry was suddenly frightened. *He's acting like Baloo*, thought Lena. Who would have expected that? Britta patted Shadow's neck, took off his saddle and bridle and watched him gallop across the clearing, buck a few times and jump over the obstacles for fun. As if on command, he reared up in the middle of the clearing and, standing on his hind legs, began whinnying loudly.

Larry watched in horror. His little hand grabbed for Britta's, and when Shadow's hooves whirled in the air he cowered behind her back.

"Don't be scared," said Britta and loosened her grip. "He doesn't eat little children for breakfast."

"No, he prefers coal-colored dogs," murmured Lena, looking at Baloo. She didn't know if she should laugh or cry.

"Whose horse is that?" Larry asked nervously.

"We borrowed it," Britta improvised quickly. "For the tournament."

Larry didn't seem to be concerned about the fact that there was a horse in a hidden garden in the middle of the woods. "But you're not allowed to ride," he said to Britta accusingly.

"This horse is the exception," she lied without blinking an eye.

Larry was so fascinated by the black horse that he forgot to ask anything else. Britta showed him the garden while Lena cleared away the tack and said goodbye to the stallion. She planted a quick kiss on Shadow's nose and gently stroked his neck. "Thank you, sweet fellow, you were fantastic today!"

On the way home, they walked with Larry between them. The little guy was totally jazzed and let Britta tell him everything about the horse. And then Lena finally had a brilliant idea to save the situation.

"Mama and Papa will get terribly upset if they hear that you went walking in the woods all by yourself. You don't want them to find out, do you?"

Larry was in the mood to believe everything. "No! Please, don't tell on me, please Lena!"

The girls looked at each other. The look on Britta's face said it all; we did it!

"Okay, Larry, We'll just forget about the fact that you snuck out after us. You were never in this part of the woods, okay?"

The boy looked from one girl to the other with a conspiratorial look in his eye. He really liked secrets. "It's a deal!"

Chapter 10

"Which horse will you be riding in the tournament today?" Mr. Bergman asked at breakfast. "Boomer?"

"No, a different horse. You don't know it yet," Lena answered evasively and quickly shoved the rest of her breakfast roll into her mouth. *After the tournament*, she promised herself. *Then I'll tell them about Shadow*.

"Don't stuff yourself like that," criticized Mrs. Bergman. "You'll get a stomachache."

"I've already got one," complained Lena. "My stomach feels like I swallowed a swarm of butterflies!"

"I want to go to the tournament, too!" cried Larry with a mouthful of cereal.

"Later," smiled Mr. Bergman. "We all want to watch Lena."

Lena glanced at her watch and jumped up hastily. "I have to get going!"

"Lena," called Mrs. Bergman from the kitchen, "you forgot your cell phone."

But Lena was already at the coat rack. "No big deal," she yapped as she slipped into her boots. The door slammed immediately thereafter. Mrs. Bergman sighed and set about doing the dishes while Larry's little fingers greedily grabbed for the cell phone.

The day was perfect for a tournament. The cloudless sky shimmered a royal blue and allowed the sun to illuminate the magnificent display of colors on the autumn leaves. Although the air was damp and cold, Lena felt happy as a clam in her Icelandic sweater. Underneath it she wore a freshly ironed dark blue sweatshirt that in her opinion looked smashing with the snow-white pants for the tournament.

Britta laughed as Lena rode up to the birch tree. "That's what you want to wear in the tournament?"

Lena looked down at her clothes. She had pulled her heavy snow pants over her freshly polished boots so that her white tournament pants wouldn't get any mud stains on them. She frowned and grabbed her friend's arm. "Come on, let's get going. We can't be late!"

Shadow seemed to sense the nervous energy in the air. He nudged the apple off Lena's hand and snorted in her face as if to say, *Hey, stay cool, you've got me!*

"Okay, all right. I have to calm down, I know. But

it's easier said than done." Lena watched Britta groom the stallion, put on his bridle and turn to look at her with anticipation.

"Did you say something?"

"I said, I have a surprise for you. Now close your eyes."

Lena obeyed and when Britta allowed her to open them again she couldn't believe her eyes. On Shadow's back lay the old English saddle, *her* saddle, but beautifully polished. And underneath it was a brand new saddle blanket with a monogram stitched on it. The elaborately stitched script letters were the initials of the name they had given their stray: Moonlight Shadow.

"Oh Britta, that's just beautiful!" Lena embraced her friend. "Now he looks like a real jumping horse. Thank you so, so much!"

Britta blushed with pride. "And now you have to win, right?"

Lena nodded enthusiastically. She took Shadow on the line and led him out of the garden. This day was a very special day; she could feel it deep down in her very soul!

"The participants for novice level jumping over here, please," commanded one of the helpers.

"Register with Sandra, please. You'll get your start number, which you'll have to attach to the brow band of your horse in such a way that it's easily visible. Darn it, where did the finish flag get to? I had it here a minute ago!" The helper looked around. Britta hurried over to her and handed her the finish flag that had fallen out of its bracket and slipped under the table.

Lena leaned on Shadow's neck and watched the stallion looking around alertly. She hardly recognized her own riding club. There were people everywhere, riders and audience were standing and walking around, and horses were whinnying as they were being unloaded from their trailers. What a crowd: parents who'd come to cheer on their kids, children who were playing hide and seek between the legs of the horses, and riders who took care of a few last minute things. In all this commotion there were also at least a dozen dogs sniffing at road apples or pulling on their leashes. Lena scanned the crowd, but she didn't see her parents anywhere.

"Lena, your start number is eighteen. Can I help you attach it?" Lena turned around and saw Sandra walking over to her. Her riding instructor looked at Shadow admiringly.

"You sure found yourself a beautiful horse!" She tied the start number to his brow band and stroked the stallion's shiny black neck. "Be careful that with all the excitement you don't forget the course!" she advised her with a wink and then walked over to the next participant.

That's all I need, thought Lena and began to warm up Shadow for the jumping. She rode a few rounds in the ring and let Shadow begin trotting. But she wasn't concentrating well since she couldn't keep her eyes off the colorful masses in front of the covered riding arena, and she nearly crashed into Boomer.

"Watch where you're going," snapped Julia. "If you try to confuse my horse, that's cheating and you're out of the tournament – got that?"

"Sorry," murmured Lena. She took up the reins and looked straight ahead as she set off again, but she felt Julia's eyes stabbing her back like a dagger.

"Hey Lena," called Ellie as she maneuvered Jasper next to the stallion. "Are you ready?"

Lena looked over at Jasper's start number – he had the 17 attached to his long brow band. She slowed Shadow down to a walk and managed to smile. "Oh, I feel like I'm going to go crazy with all this excitement!"

"I just sang Jasper a good luck song so that he'll jump well later. Do you want to hear it? I'm sure it'll help." She hummed a melody off-key and Lena had to laugh.

"You'd better stop right now or you'll chase the audience away!"

Ellie frowned and trotted toward the practice obstacle. The gelding obediently jumped without the slightest hesitation. Satisfied, Ellie nodded. "You see? My good luck song. It wouldn't surprise me if we win today."

Lena felt the nervousness in her stomach start up again when Sandra stepped into the ring to call the first starter to take her place. Unfortunately she couldn't see the course from the practice area, but the first starter had an unhappy expression on her face as she rode out of the arena afterwards. The loudspeaker announced, "That was the first starter with a 12-fault ride."

"There aren't even that many obstacles," Ellie said in amazement.

"Silly goose," said Lena, "for every knockdown the judges count four faults. So if you make a fault on three obstacles, then the result is 12 faults."

"Oh, I see," nodded Ellie, "The rider with the fewest fault points is the winner. But what happens if more than one rider has the same number of points?"

"Then it's decided on time," explained Lena. "The best riders start again against each other – that's called a jump-off. The winner is the rider who has the fewest faults and the fastest time.

The next rider disappeared into the arena and Lena cocked her ears. Sometimes she heard a long "Ooooh," from the audience, and then suddenly the sound of loud applause would drift outside. Shadow got increasingly agitated and Lena had to exert herself to keep him calm.

Finally it was Ellie's turn. She stroked Jasper's mane, winked at Lena and quietly hummed her lucky song as she rode into the arena. "Good luck," Lena wished her friend and crossed her fingers for her. Her stomach simply refused to calm down so she tried the practice obstacle one more time and then took her place near the area exit. She would have to ride into the course right after Ellie. *Will I do everything right? Which obstacle comes after the oxer, the vertical or the wall? Should I slow Shadow down or should I just let him keep his tempo for jumping?* The thoughts swirled wildly around in her head and Lena wished her ride was already over.

Laughter drifted out of the arena, and then the audience clapped long and loud. Lena's stomach was in a flurry from the excitement, and then Jasper's head emerged from the door opening. Ellie had bright red cheeks and shook her head, laughing. "We totally blew it – three refusals!"

Lena let her friend pass, and then she steered Shadow into the arena. Britta stood at the entrance and smiled encouragingly. "Good luck, you two!"

Lena pulled in her head and rode into the course, her heart pounding.

The telephone range twice, three times. Then a squeaky child's voice answered, "Larry Bergman!"

The man frowned and furrowed his brow in bewilderment. He cleared his throat and said, "I'm looking for Lena Bergman."

"Not here," squeaked the little fellow cheerfully.

"When will she return?" Impatiently, the man drummed his fingers on the dashboard. Darn it, he should have just asked to speak with the parents right away. What did a little kid like that know anyway?

"Dunno," mumbled Larry. "When the tournament is over."

Taking note, the man prodded, "Tournament? What kind of tournament?"

"At the riding club," said Larry good-naturedly. "She's been riding there a long time. And today she'll be jumping with a gigantic black horse!"

Bingo. A victorious smile appeared on the man's face. "Where is the riding club?" he asked in a slightly friendlier voice.

"Behind the church steeple," giggled Larry.

The man looked out of the car window. He could just make out the church steeple at the other end of the village, standing behind the tall pine trees. He turned the key in the ignition and then hung up without saying good-bye.

"Next at the start is Lena Bergman on Moonlight Shadow." The announcement resonated from the loudspeaker, startling Lena, who winced. She quickly pulled herself together and greeted the judges and waited for the signal to start. Shadow seemed to know what the signal meant, because he took the bit between his teeth and galloped off. *I have no idea anymore which obstacle comes first*, Lena thought in a panic. Then she suddenly saw the nicely painted vertical with the number 1 directly in front of her. From then on she needed to do nothing more than guide the stallion in the right direction. Shadow took every jump willingly and easily. His hooves never even came close to the poles, and Lena enjoyed her ride so much that she was almost disappointed when thunderous applause erupted. She breathlessly slowed the stallion to a walk.

"That was the first no-fault ride of the day, ladies and gentlemen. Applause for Lena Bergman on Moonlight Shadow!"

Britta and Ellie stormed Lena when she was back outside in the sunlight. "Terrific job, Lena! That was the best ride so far!"

"I didn't do anything," Lena admitted happily. "Shadow jumped by himself!"

Lena barely took note of the next two riders, but then she quickly jumped down from the horse and pressed the reins into Britta's hand. "Can you hold on to him please? I'd like to watch Julia." She followed behind the nervously prancing Boomer until the entryway to the arena and then observed agitatedly how he made a startled little hop at every little noise. Julia struggled just to get him to canter toward the first obstacle, but once he made it over he started to enjoy himself. Although he performed the craziest bucks in between obstacles, he finished the course fault-free and reaped enthusiastic applause.

"Well, will there be a jump-off?" Britta asked in the din of the loud applause.

"Yes," Lena frowned. "Boomer jumped wonderfully."

"Should I sing my good luck song for you?" Ellie offered. "Then you'll win for sure!"

After the last rider had finished, their riding teacher called Lena and Julia over to explain the rules for a jump-off. "Okay, now there are only six jumps. They have to be taken fault-free and as fast as possible in the correct order. If both of you manage to complete the course fault-free, then the time will decide the winner. Is that clear?"

Lena nodded, and Julia did likewise.

"Then we'll draw straws for the order." Sandra held two straws between her fingers. Lena guessed what would happen and promptly drew the shorter straw.

"Okay, then Julia will begin. Good luck to you both!"

Lena got back into Shadow's saddle and began to trot with him in the outside ring while Julia rode onto the course with Boomer. *This is my big chance*, thought Lena excitedly – *it's now or never!* She took up the reins and tried not to pay attention to the noises coming from the audience. *Just stay calm,* she told herself. *The most important thing is to stay fault-free. The time is secondary. There – was that just applause?* Lena sighed, bit her lip and listened. At the entrance to the hall, she discovered her parents and her brother excitedly waving to her.

Enthusiastic applause erupted and Julia rode out of the course, beaming. Her eye caught Lena's and a wide grin appeared on her face. "Today is not a good day for you, Lena."

Shadow pranced and Lena chewed on her lip as she rode past Boomer in the narrow entryway to the arena. Her heart was pounding like crazy and her knees were shaking. It wasn't until she approached the first obstacle that she felt the tension dissipate. Once again she allowed Shadow to take the lead. The stallion shot out and simply flew over the poles. He unerringly took the second and third obstacles, made a bold turn, and leapt over the fourth and fifth obstacles with the grace of a cat. Lena saw the wall fly before them and noticed that it had been raised in order to make the jump-off more exciting. *Just one more jump*, she thought, and inside she was already cheering. *We were so fast! Just the wall, and then we've done it. Then we've won!*

Shadow galloped toward the wall with powerful strides until it disappeared from his view. No obstacle was too high for him at this moment, because for the first time in his life he felt the pure joy of jumping. But then just as his muscles prepared to push off and his vision began to blur, he saw the man. His bald head and his evil grin had stalked the stallion ever since that horrible night, and the flames kept threatening to burn his coat. Suddenly it was as if he was back in the shed again, trapped, surrounded by flames, and he felt hot and cold at the same time. No longer able to control himself, his legs gave out and his tensed body gave up, tearing away from the audience where the evil was hiding. He heard a scream as the flyweight slipped out of his saddle, and then he snapped out of his fit with a sudden clarity and remembered who he was – and who was sitting on his back. As quickly as it had come, the fit was over. Shadow stood still, his flanks shaking. Had his eyes been playing tricks on him?

"Lena," a voice called out over the din, "wouldn't you like to complete the course?"

Lena caught Sandra's eye and saw that she was nodding encouragingly at her. Refused. The thought shot through her head. We lost.

It was completely silent in the arena, as though the audience was holding its breath, waiting to see what Lena would do. She felt her hands take up the reins again, her body straighten up in the saddle, and her legs guide Shadow in a circle, back into the lane to the unlucky wall. The stallion snorted loudly, as the wall were a ghost, but this time he jumped so high that it seemed he had wings attached to his hooves.

Lena needed an entire round before she could halt the thundering momentum. Stunned, she steered toward the exit and rode out of the arena. Excited voices encircled her as she slipped out of the saddle, still shaking.

"Is everything okay?"

"That looked horrible!"

"What happened in there?"

Lena leaned against the stallion's quivering flank and closed her eyes for a moment. She hadn't completed the course fault-free. Julia was the winner. She was so disappointed that she wanted to cry. But that wouldn't have been fair, so she swallowed the stale feeling and smiled bravely.

"He balked suddenly. I don't know why. Everything was under control until we got to the wall!"

Mr. and Mrs. Bergman lunged for their daughter and embraced her with relief.

"Sweetheart, what was that? I thought you'd fly over the wall in a high arc! What kind of a horse is that, anyway?"

Lena and Britta exchanged glances. Lena took a deep breath. "I have to tell you something …"

But she wasn't able to finish because Sandra came over, followed by Julia and her friends.

"Come quickly, Lena! You have to ride in to the arena for the awards ceremony. After all, you came in second."

Lena nodded. She quickly jumped in the saddle before her nervous stomach could protest. When she saw Julia's gloating grin a terrible thought suddenly occurred to her. She quickly bent down to Britta. "Britta, is it possible that Julia did something to make him balk? Did you see her when we were riding the course?"

Britta was shocked and took a deep breath. "No, but even if she did, there's no way that we could prove it."

"I'll be right back," she called to her parents, then rode in to the arena for the third time that day.

"The winner of the show jumping receives a blue ribbon; Julia Steiner on Boomer!"

The audience applauded enthusiastically and Boomer, startled, jerked his head up as the fluttering ribbon came closer. Lena gave the young gelding a loving glance and applauded as well.

"In second place is Lena Bergman on Moonlight Shadow!" Again the audience applauded and Shadow, once again placid calm personified, gallantly lowered his head to allow the red ribbon to be attached. Out of the corner of her eye Lena saw that Julia did not applaud, while Sandra, Britta and Ellie cheered. Suddenly she felt bad that she had been so disappointed. She bent forward until her lips nearly touched Shadow's perked ears. "It doesn't matter at all to me that we didn't win," she whispered. "You jumped wonderfully. Thanks for everything." She patted and stroked his black neck and let her fingers glide through his shimmering mane. Shadow peered up at her and Lena convinced herself that he understood every word.

When she straightened up, she noticed that Julia had a nasty smile on her face. "Who would have thought that even with such a wonderful horse you still wouldn't manage to beat me?"

"And who would have that that you would be such a poor sport," Lena commented quietly. "I clapped for Boomer."

"That makes sense," Julia snipped. "After all, he won."

Boomer ran the ensuing lap of honor in a hunting gallop and Lena had her hands full trying to keep Shadow calm. She was thoroughly out of breath by the time she managed to slow the stallion down enough to let him walk on slackened reins. Hands stretched out to them from all sides, waiting to stroke Shadow and pat his neck. Someone even held a sugar cube under his nose. Lena was happy when they were finally out of sight.

Once outside, the sun received them with a warm smile and Lena sighed happily. She put a hand on Shadow's neck, and for a moment she forget the world around her.

"Hey, you," growled a harsh voice behind her. "Get off my horse!"

Lena winced. She felt as if someone had just thrown a bucket of cold water over her head when she realized what those words meant. Her arms and legs did not want to obey, but she slowly got down from the saddle and, with quivering fingers, held on to Shadow's mane.

Behind her stood a short, stocky man with a brown hat on his head and an angry furrowed brow over his deep-set eyes. He held a flyer in his hand with the caption *Stray horse found!* Lena felt her heart get heavy.

"Are you his owner?" She asked in a quivering voice.

"That's right," grumbled the man. "So give him to me now!"

Lena swallowed. "Could I … please, could we say goodbye to him, my friend and I?" She felt the tears shoot into her eyes, although the last thing she wanted was to cry in front of this stranger.

"Whatever," growled the man unkindly. "My trailer is back there. I'll wait exactly five minutes and then I'm driving off!"

Shadow suddenly seemed sleepy, as if all the excitement had worn him out. His eyelids grew heavy and his mouth practically hung to the ground. Lena worried as she looked him over, but the strange man didn't seem upset. He grabbed the reins with a hard grip and led the stallion to his trailer. Shadow followed him meekly and Lena ran off to look for Britta.

She found her friend in the arena where she was rearranging the obstacles for the more difficult jumping course. She waved excitedly.

"Come quickly – there's a man who wants to take Shadow away!"

Curious glances followed the girls as they ran back to the horse trailer. Shadow was already tied up inside the trailer. The barrier was shut, but the loading ramp was still down. Without wasting another thought, Lena rushed in and embraced Shadow's black neck. Britta

133

went in next to her and gently stroked his soft coat one more time.

"I'll never forget you," Lena whispered as the man stuck his head in behind them and cleared his throat impatiently. Britta tugged at her sleeve and they slinked down the ramp backwards.

He looks sad, thought Lena, and a heavy lump lodged in her throat. *We'll probably never see him again.*

"Where are you taking him?" Britta asked quickly. "Could we come to visit him?"

"Oh sure," the man grinned and waved the flyer. "I have your names and telephone numbers – I'll just give you a call!"

They watched as the SUV with the horse trailer maneuvered its way out of the parking area before disappearing down the road, its motor wailing. *Just like the morning after a nice dream,* thought Lena. *Now we've woken up.*

In the middle of the parking area lay their saddle, which the unfriendly man had tossed to the ground thoughtlessly. Lena felt a piercing in her heart as her gaze landed on the monogram stitched into the saddle blanket. She lifted it up and hugged the leather to her. It was still warm and soft from Shadow's steaming back.

"What just happened?" Sandra crossed the parking area and looked uncomprehendingly from the saddle in Lena's arms to her eyes and back again. "Did he run away from you?"

Lena waved to her parents. Then she sunk onto a bench with the saddle still in her arms and began to tell what happened in a quivering voice. She didn't dare look up, especially not into the faces of her parents. She quickly got the facts out. When she finished, she was shocked to see that half of her riding club was standing around looking at her and Britta with unbelieving eyes. The worst was the silent accusation on her mother's face.

Mr. Bergman cleared his throat and stood up. "Well, that surely was a hair-raising tale. Do you have any idea what kind of trouble you could be in?"

Lena bit her lip. "But Shadow is back with his owner."

"That's not what I'm talking about!" Mr. Bergman shook his head at the depths of their irrationality. "You can't just keep a horse that doesn't belong to you, ride him and participate in tournaments! Stand up, both of you. We're going right now!"

To Shadow? Lena wanted to ask hopefully, but the look in her father's eyes smoldered and she kept her mouth shut.

Mr. Berman pulled the car key out of his pocket and handed it to his wife. "Here, take Larry to the neighbors. Drive over to Mrs. Sutherland and tell her everything. I'll take a taxi with the girls and drive on ahead. We'll meet at the police station!"

136

Appalled, Lena and Britta exchanged glances. "Police ...?"

"What were you thinking," Mr. Bergman shouted angrily, "just keeping a strange horse? Who knows? There may already be a police report out against you!"

The air in the police station was stuffy and smelled like dusty files. In between modern flat computer screens they saw clunky black telephones with fat keys sitting on old-fashioned desks, which were covered in stacks of handwritten reports, black and white mug shots and stained brown coffee cups.

Lena reached automatically for Britta's hand when they had to follow a bearded policeman into an interrogation room and sit down at a beat-up wooden table. They felt like dangerous criminals, even though their eyes were burning with tears that hadn't yet fallen.

Mr. Bergman began with an explanation, but the policeman shook his head and explained that he wanted to hear the story from the girls themselves. So they told, in turn, about the night in the woods, the secret garden, the rides in the clearing. They talked until their mouths went dry and their tongues stuck to the roof of their mouths and they couldn't find any more words to describe their black friend.

"So this is about a stray horse that came to you." The policeman turned on the monitor that was standing on the table and pecked at the keyboard. "There we have it. Do you recognize this animal?"

He turned the screen so that the girls could see the photograph that was clearly of Shadow. But under the picture there was another name: *Black Diamond*.

"Is that his name?" Britta asked carefully.

"Exactly. The horse was stolen two weeks ago out of a tournament box belonging to the Von Bernheims."

Mrs. Bergman sucked in air in shock.

"It's puzzling to us how he could get to this area," continued the policeman as he gave the adults a conciliatory look, "because this stable is pretty far up north. We now suspect that he escaped from thieves."

"But you don't believe that our daughters stole the horse?" blustered Mr. Bergman.

"Of course not." The policeman shook his head and turned the monitor back. "It says here that the owner, Mrs. Von Bernheim, believes that professional horse thieves must have been involved."

"Mrs. Von Bernheim?" Lena raised her eyebrows. "But it was a man who picked him up."

"Then it must have been one of her employees," guessed the policeman and paged through the electronic file. "Mrs. Von Bernheim will be pleased when she gets her horse back – it caused quite a commotion when he disappeared."

"But why didn't anyone look for him then?" Britta asked, full of surprise.

"Horses that disappear don't usually just reappear

again," explained the policeman. "We recommended to the owners that they report the loss to their insurers and look for a new horse."

"And is that what Shadow's...I mean, Black Diamond's owner did?" Lena was shocked, and thought, *If Shadow had been my horse, I would never have given up without a fight. I would have done everything I could to find him again!*

"Of course," the policeman nodded. "That horse is extremely valuable. He was insured for almost two million!"

Britta's jaw fell open and Lena had to steady herself in her chair. "Wow," she whispered breathlessly. "That's a lot of money!"

"He had the best papers and was descended from a famous jumping horse," the policeman read out from his file and smiled gently at the girls. "Looks like you made quite a catch, you two."

"But," Britta began and furrowed her brow, "if he's so famous, why didn't anybody recognize him? In the tournament or in all the stables where we hung up our flyers?"

The policeman shrugged his shoulders and scanned the computer screen. "It says here that the horse was not very successful in jumping. He won a few promising new talent prizes, but then his performance declined so much that he couldn't even place anymore."

139

"Just think, I rode in a club tournament with a genuine jumping horse!" Lena had to giggle, although she didn't feel much like laughing. More like crying. *Why?* she thought. *Why can't Shadow just be a normal farm horse? They maybe we could keep him. But a valuable jumping horse ...*

"For you girls, the case is now closed." The policeman made a note in his file, added something to his handwritten log and pushed it over to Lena's parents and Mrs. Sutherland so that they could sign it.

"Does that mean that we won't get in trouble for keeping the horse?" Lena asked timidly.

The policeman shook his head and smiled. "No. You did try to find the right owner. Besides, you didn't steal the horse. And on top of that, you took good care of him." He gave Mr. and Mrs. Bergman and Mrs. Sutherland an earnest look. "You shouldn't punish the girls. They probably saved the horse's life."

"And what about the garden?" Britta smiled lopsidedly. "We broke the lock."

"Old Kramer's garden?" the policeman laughed out loud. "You're in luck, because no one will make you answer for that, either. The owners aren't alive anymore and no one has bothered to tear the old fence down."

Lena's parents were visibly relieved when they were allowed to leave the interrogation room. Britta tugged on Lena's sleeve and held her back. They waited until the policeman had locked the room and looked at him uncertainly.

"What will happen now with Shad ... with Black Diamond?" Britta asked quietly.

"He's probably already home again in his own stable." The policeman put his big hands on their shoulders and led them in the direction of the exit. "We'll tell the owner who found her horse. Then she can thank you herself."

"But ..." Lena started.

"Don't worry." The policeman looked at them sternly. "We'll see to it that everything is in order." He took out the police log and handed it to another policeman. "Here, send two officers over. They should check to make sure that the stolen horse is back safe and sound." Then he turned back to the girls. "Okay, you two go home now and ..."

A telephone rang and the policeman yelled out, "That's mine!" He hectically ran around the desk, grabbed the receiver and turned around so that Lena couldn't hear anything.

But she could read; the piece of paper had the address of Shadow's owner. She repeated the words to herself for a long time, until they were permanently burned into her memory. Then she followed Britta, who was gesticulating wildly.

Chapter 11

The black stallion stood jammed in next to the barrier wall, oozing merciless pearls of sweat underneath the thick wool blanket. Where were they bringing him this time? He recognized the trailer, which had been his permanent companion to all the tournaments. But his instinct warned him, whistled in his ears and sent a hot-cold shudder down his spine.

Something was wrong.

Shadow whinnied with restraint. His new friends had just been with him, but why weren't they here now? Why had they allowed him to be taken away again? And why, for heaven's sake, did he feel so horribly feeble and sleepy? He stood like this on his trip into the unknown for quite some time. He clearly sensed danger; he could smell it, even taste it. Finally the SUV came to a noisy stop. Doors slammed, and then the small opening next to his head was thrown open. The stallion's body was flooded with a sense of panic. He looked around, let his gaze scan the walls and the raised ramp and knew in that moment that all was lost. Trapped, surrendered. Then he saw the needle that the man filled. He had seen that once before, felt that once before.

Shadow let out a bloodcurdling whinny, like a single hopeless cry for help.

Ellie jumped up when she saw her friends leave the police station. The girls embraced.

"Sandra drove here with me," Ellie reported quietly. "We wanted to know what happened."

Lena looked cautiously over to her parents. She didn't know whether the thunder that she expected would come immediately or if her father would wait until they had gotten home.

"You're lucky that the police saw your behavior as nothing more than thoughtless dreaming," Mr. Berman began. "What's left are your lies and your bad grades, Lena. For that you're grounded for two weeks, and for the remainder of the school year we'll be monitoring your homework."

Lena nodded timidly. "Believe me, I really only wanted …"

Her father interrupted her. "Even if you just wanted to help the horse, you should have taken it to a real stable instead of keeping it. That was truly thoughtless of you."

"Just think what could have happened!" Mrs. Sutherland pressed her lips into a thin line. "I just can't believe that you rode that strange horse, Britta!"

"I'm sorry," exclaimed Britta. Her face was ashen and she looked miserable. "I just wanted to finally be able to ride."

"When you're eighteen, you can do and not do whatever you want," said Mrs. Sutherland curtly. "As long as I'm responsible for you, you will not risk your life on one of those unpredictable animals."

"But I can't wait! The longer I wait …" Britta's breath came in spurts and gasps and Lena heard her trying to repress a sob. "You infect me with your fears, don't you see that?"

Sandra took a step forward. "Mrs. Sutherland, please excuse me for getting involved, but your daughter is right. It's much easier for children to learn a sport. If Britta has to wait until she's an adult, she'll never ride as confidently as Lena, for example."

Mrs. Sutherland looked at the riding instructor aghast. "And what if something were to happen to her? What if she fell or the animal kicked at her with its hooves …?"

"I can assure you that at our riding school we only have well trained horses," Sandra said quickly. "And I would personally see to it that Britta receives solid training."

Mrs. Sutherland looked in her daughter's eyes and suddenly her lips bent into a smile. "I'll think it over," she said with hesitation. "But if I were to say yes, then I would only allow it with a riding helmet and safety vest."

Britta squealed and embraced her mother tightly.

"Can we finally go home now?" Mrs. Bergman looked impatiently at her wristwatch.

Lena and Britta exchanged glances. "Can't we just see if Shadow is doing okay?" she asked carefully.

"Lena, I think you've done enough today …" her father thundered.

"Please!" Lena hugged her father and then grabbed his arm tightly. "Please please please, daddy. If he's there and he's okay, then I swear that you'll never hear me say another word about him. You can even ground me for four weeks! But please, let's drive over there!"

"Lena, it's just not possible," Mrs. Bergman interrupted. "I have to pick up Larry, and Baloo is home all alone."

Sandra raised her hands. "I could drive."

"You?" Mrs. Bergman looked at the riding instructor dubiously. "Why should you?"

"Well, I'm curious about this fantastic tournament stable," she said and winked at the girls. "Besides, the stallion really impressed me. I'd like to know that he's doing okay after the girls took care of him for so long."

The adults exchanged glances, first dubious, then full of understanding. In the end, Mr. Bergman nodded and shook off his daughter from his arm.

"Alright then. With adult supervision I'll allow it. But as soon as you've seen the horse you'll have to come back, is that clear?"

"Yes sir," Lena promised and gave her father another hug.

Naturally Ellie squeezed in next to Lena in the backseat of Sandra's VW Rabbit.

"Where do we have to go, anyway?" asked Sandra. Britta told her the address that was on the paper and Sandra groaned. "That's not exactly just around the corner, people. Alright, then, what do you say we make a quick stop at McDonald's first and I'll buy us some provisions?"

The sun had already begun its descent and hung low in the brilliant afternoon sky when the little Rabbit turned into the stately lane. Pebbles flew up as the car's squeaky brakes brought it to a stop. A police car was already parked next to the giant chestnut tree in the middle of a grand courtyard.

The girls timidly got out of the car and stretched their legs, stiff from the long drive. Lena looked around. In front of them a pebbled walkway snaked through a well-tended flower garden to an immaculate looking manor house of enormous proportions. To the left was a jumping ring. It was surrounded by a thick hedge to prevent any casual passerby from looking in. To the right stood a magnificent whitewashed stable. They didn't have the slightest doubt that this was the right house, because the green wooden gate had been left wide open and afforded a view of the spacious boxes in the dim interior.

Lena felt a strange sensation in her stomach. Was she about to see Shadow again?

"Strange horse farm," Ellie said, her voice just a whisper, although there wasn't another person to be seen anywhere. "Aren't there any paddocks around here?"

"I saw a few enclosures behind the stable," Sandra whispered back. "I have a feeling that the horses are only here to work."

Ellie and Britta looked around doubtfully; Sandra walked over to the police car and peeked into the interior. The doors were locked and the car stood there as if abandoned. "They'll have to come back some time," she said reassuringly.

Lena walked around in circles, each time getting a little closer to the stable entrance, her hands buried deep in the pockets of her Icelandic sweater. She ambled here and there, seemingly without a plan, through the pebbled courtyard. With her gaze lowered, she peered at the others with one eye. Ellie looked around her, and Britta and Sandra were conversing in a whisper about something in the police car. Nobody paid attention to her. As if by pure chance, her little stroll led her to the stable entrance. "No trespassing!" was written on one of the yellow warning signs. She looked over her shoulder one more time to be sure the others weren't following her. Ellie was leaning over Britta's shoulders. The three had discovered something interesting in the police car. Lena held her breath and carefully sneaked a peek just inside the dark stable. From her vantage point on her side of the bars in front of the boxes, she only saw the vague outline of a few horses. There didn't seem to be a single person inside. She quickly slipped in the door and then pressed her back against the cold stone wall behind it.

The stable was damp and poorly ventilated. The door probably wasn't open very often. Lena waited for her eyes to adjust to the low level of light and then looked around again. She found herself in a generously designed stable, with four giant boxes on either side and another eight in the center aisle. The ceiling was quite low, which made the space seem smaller than it was. Still, the entire stable looked clean and well kept: no spider webs clung to the corners, not a single bird's nest perched atop on any of the beams. Lena wasn't sure why, but she felt a thousand times more comfortable in a homey wooden stable, with a healthy dose of horse dirt and bugs than in this sterile, oppressive cleanliness.

At the other end of the center aisle she heard steps.

Whoever it was came out from behind the opposite box and wouldn't discover Lena until he got around the corner.

Was that a policeman? And if not, who?

Lena looked around and spied a stack of hay directly next to the box she stood in front of. She quickly slipped behind the hay and ducked down, just in case. When the footsteps came nearer, Lena carefully peeked out from behind the hay, and suddenly held her breath. It was the stranger from the tournament! Although he wasn't wearing a hat anymore, Lena was almost certain she recognized Shadow's driver. She was overcome with relief – if the man was here, then that could only mean that Shadow was here, too. But the man didn't walk into the courtyard; instead he remained in the dark stable and peeked outside. Suddenly he cursed quietly, turned around and quickly walked back in the direction he had come from.

Only after his footsteps had faded away completely did Lena dare to come out of her hiding place. She tried to eavesdrop, but couldn't hear another thing. Instead, however, she heard voices in the courtyard – the policemen had probably returned to their car. Lena scurried down the alley in front of her. She peeked into the boxes on either side and looked into the friendly horse eyes that looked back at her with curiosity. Most of the animals were chestnuts, but there was also a white horse among them. But no black horses – and no Shadow. And there was no empty box that could belong to him.

Lena sneaked back along the inner side of the alley and dared to go on tiptoe to the opposite side where the man had disappeared. She stayed tight along the sides of the boxes and peeked around the corner for quite some time before she went down the second alley. Two dark horses stood there, but neither of them was the stallion she was searching for. Lena walked a little further and attentively looked over the horses behind the bars. She stopped in front of the last box. It was empty – but on the door hung a brass sign with a fancy inscription: *Black Diamond*.

Lena gaped at the box as though she believed that Shadow would suddenly appear out of nowhere if only she looked long enough. Suddenly she felt a gust of air. She felt boiling hot because it occurred to her that there was still a man hiding in here. He must have gone out the back! Lena looked at the wall and discovered a narrow door that fit unobtrusively in the wall. As if on cue, she heard voices coming from behind the door. The people whose voices she heard were arguing loudly and one of them seemed to be the bald man.

Lena stumbled backwards. Panicked, she felt along behind her for a place to hide, but her fingers touched nothing but the rough wooden walls. *I have to get into Shadow's box!* She thought frantically. She turned her back to the stable wall, searched for the bolt and pushed the door open. She quickly slipped into the box, reached through the bars and pulled the bolt closed again. She managed to disappear behind the wooden wall just in time before the door in the stable wall flew open with a crash.

Outside in the courtyard, the haggard figure of a long-haired man appeared, emerging from the manor house. He came down the path between two policemen and three pairs of eyes focused on the unexpected visitors who had taken their position next to the old chestnut tree.

"May I help you?" The long-haired man, who had his hair gathered into a ponytail, raised his eyebrows and didn't exactly look friendly.

"Good evening," Sandra greeted him politely. "We just came to see about the stallion."

"Black Diamond? The stolen horse?" The long-haired man seemed utterly confused and exchanged glances with both policemen. "What's going on here, anyway? Is this a nasty game of hide and seek?"

The smaller of the two policemen cleared his throat. "I'm very sorry, but there must be a misunderstanding. Who are you anyway?" He looked at Sandra and the two girls, and there was a certain severity in his gaze.

"We found Shadow … er, Black Diamond," Britta blurted. "He strayed to us in the woods."

"Oh, you're the ones." The taller policeman nodded understandingly and suddenly looked a lot friendlier. "This is an excellent coincidence."

"Listen, we really don't want to bother you," Sandra said conciliatorily. "Could we possibly see the horse briefly … so that the girls can say goodbye to him?"

"That won't be possible," the long-haired man interrupted her rudely. Then he turned back to the policemen. "Gentlemen, we should really wait for Mrs. Von Bernheim before we speak any further about this."

Ellie nudged Britta and motioned to the empty courtyard around them.

"Hey – where's Lena, anyway?"

Britta looked around in fright. "Oh, no," she mumbled and her gaze focused on the long stable building. "She probably wanted to see Shadow!"

The long-haired man squinted and looked over toward the yellow no trespassing sign meaningfully. The smaller policeman stepped forward quickly. "No reason for excitement, Mr. Hansen. I'm sure the girl will be right back." He turned to Sandra and the girls. "The stallion never turned up here."

Someone stomped through the stable in heavy boots.

"What were you thinking, Karl?"

Lena shuddered. She didn't recognize this other voice, but it sounded cold and unpredictable. And it clearly belonged to a woman.

"I'll put things in order again," bald-headed Karl promised her.

"I take it you are aware of whom Hansen is talking with out there," hissed the woman. "The police apparently claim that our stolen horse has reappeared. I trust you understand what that means."

"The insurance company won't pay the money," Karl grumbled so quietly that Lena had to hold her breath in order to hear better. "And if you don't get your money, then I don't get my money."

"Exactly," barked the woman. Her voice shook in anger. "That useless nag has cost us the most expensive fodder for years, and how does he thank us? Not a single tournament victory, not even the smallest prize! His disappearance is our only chance to turn his excellent papers into money. Have you finally comprehended just what's at stake here?"

"I'll put things in order again," Karl promised her again. Lena pressed her body even tighter against the wall of the box and prayed that neither of them would look into the empty box.

"I swear, Karl, if you blow it again …"

"No, no." The bald man lowered his voice. "I've taken precautions. This time nothing will go wrong, believe me. I increased the dosage of the tranquilizer again. That black horse's hours are numbered."

Suddenly it was so quiet in the stable that Lena wanted to raise her head and look around, but the woman only seemed to be listening to what was happening in the courtyard. Karl wheezed quietly and Lena pressed herself against the wall and hardly dared to breathe.

"They're back. I have to go."

"You can count on me, Mrs. Von Bernheim," Karl called after her, as her hollow steps on the concrete floor grew fainter. For a while he seemed to think about something. Then he grabbed an object that was apparently hanging on the wall and pushed the back door open again. "Well, might as well get it over with now," he grumbled. Then the door shut quietly and Karl's footsteps crunched through the pebbles.

Lena took a careful breath and listened. She was alone again. As she slowly stood up and reached out through the bars to slide open the bolt she noticed that her hands were shaking. Her entire body felt like she had bathed in ice water, but the horrible feeling of cold seemed to come from inside of her.

Shadow, she thought. *They were talking about Shadow!* She shook her head to chase away the horrible thought that had been planted in her brain. Nobody had stolen Shadow. They had gotten rid of him in order to cash in the insurance policy on him – that was fraud! And the mastermind of the whole sinister operation was none other than Mrs. Von Bernheim, the owner of this grand tournament stable – and of Black Diamond!

Lena's vision chased her thoughts from the back door in the stable to the direction of the courtyard where the crook was talking to the policemen. *There isn't enough time to explain everything,* she thought desperately. *By the time they finally believe me, that Karl will be long gone! And then it'll probably be too late for Shadow…*

The door in the wall was only leaned shut. Lena looked back one more time, and then she carefully grabbed the handle, pulled the door open and peeked out. In front of her were a few fenced in paddocks. The sandy ground was churned up and muddy and there was not a single blade of grass.

There was no sign of the bald man.

Lena slipped outside and pulled the door closed behind her. She crept along as close to the wall as possible in order to be able to hide quickly in case the man suddenly came around the corner, but nothing happened. What did happen is that she suddenly heard someone singing quietly. Lena stopped at the corner of the stable and carefully peered around to the other side. Karl stood in front of the new SUV that he had used a few hours earlier to pick up Shadow with the horse trailer. The door was open and the radio played rock music.

Lena quickly pulled her head back out of fear that Karl might discover her. She took cover behind a pile of boards and tucked in her head.

Karl seemed to be loading something into the car. The trunk clicked, and then she heard the crunch of his rubber soles in the pebbles.

"How could that have happened? Darn it anyway!"

Karl slammed the trunk again and came toward Lena with big steps. Frightened, she held her breath, but Karl walked past her and disappeared into a small shed where a tractor was parked.

Lena's thoughts raced. Was it possible…but how else would they ever find Shadow?

She took a deep breath and slipped out of her hiding spot. She looked back at the shed, but Karl hadn't left it yet. She quickly dashed around the corner of the stable toward the SUV. She hesitated for a second, but then the image popped into her head of Shadow, tied up and helpless, burning to death in a sea of flames, and her fear evaporated. Lena peered into the car. The key was in the ignition, which meant that Karl would be back any minute! She pushed aside all those thoughts and opened the back car door. There was a tarp on the back seat – that would have to be enough to conceal her. She quickly climbed into the car and pulled the door closed as noiselessly as possible.

When Karl returned and started up the car, Lena lay crouching underneath the tarp, wondering how long the journey would take.

Chapter 12

Mrs. Von Bernheim wore her hair pulled back in a severe looking bun. She had clean leather riding boots on her feet and her elegant breeches looked as if they had never come in contact with a saddle before.

"Thank you for going to the trouble of driving all the way out here to us," she smiled and extended a thin hand to the two policemen. "My estate manager must have showed you around and discussed the details with you."

"Well, coincidentally, this woman and these girls turned up here as well," the taller policemen interjected. "They found your missing horse."

"Is that so?" Mrs. Von Bernheim raised her eyebrows and looked over Britta and Ellie with disdain. "And are you certain that it was my horse? I mean, are you even capable of recognizing that the animal in question was a valuable Thoroughbred stallion?"

"The girls identified him on the basis of the photograph," explained the smaller policeman.

"Ah, and where is this horse now?" Mrs. Von Bernheim crossed her arms in front of her chest and frowned. She looked as if she had bitten a slice of sour lemon.

"A man picked it up," Britta explained shyly. "A man with a brown hat, and he claimed that the horse belonged to him."

"Well, there are many horses that fit his description," the posh woman waved them aside. "Did you ask to see his ID? Or the papers for the horse?"

"Uh, no…" Britta stammered timidly. Sandra came to her aid and laid her arm protectively around her shoulder. "The girls were far too upset for that. Listen to me ..."

"No, you listen to me," Mrs. Von Bernheim shook her head gruffly. "I'm a businesswoman. I can't waste my time with emotional outbursts, so I will have to ask you and your two girls to leave my farm. The horse is not here; the gentlemen from the police have already seen that for themselves. All of us have a strenuous day of work ahead of us."

Britta shared a disappointed look with Sandra. The entire long trip – was it all for nothing?

"Excuse me, but that's not possible." Ellie turned bright red with anger and the unfamiliar woman stared into her face as though she had a disgusting insect sitting on the tip of her nose. "We can't drive home yet."

"Oh?" she asked in a sugary sweet voice, "and why not?"

Ellie stretched her arms out and twirled in a circle.

"Well, because Lena has disappeared! If the horse isn't here, then why hasn't she come back?"

Lena had to periodically lift the tarp she was lying under in order to get enough air. Every time she did, she looked ahead. The longer they drove, the more desolate the area looked, and the more frightened Lena became. The sky had already gone gray; soon it would be completely dark.

Karl whistled aimlessly for a while. Then he turned on the radio and sang extremely off-key with familiar songs. He had trouble with the SUV's stick shift and cursed loudly every time the car made a sudden lurch. Each time, Lena had to be careful that she didn't get thrown forward or the tarp didn't fall off to reveal the stowaway.

They had already driven for about half an hour. Lena was so frightened that she hardly dared to breathe. What had she been thinking? If Karl really were ruthless enough to kill a horse, then he wouldn't be afraid to do something to her as well. Still, at this point, there was no turning back.

Lena carefully felt in her jacket pocket. When her fingers failed the find anything, she felt ice-cold shock; her cell phone wasn't there! In her mind's eye, she saw it lying on the kitchen table that morning. Lena felt like slapping herself for being so dumb. Now she couldn't even call for help! But even if she could, what would she tell the others? That she was in a criminal's car, driving along on some country road? Something else alarmed her: she didn't have the slightest idea where she was. What if Karl were to stop somewhere in the wilderness? Would she be able to make it to the next town? Assuming that she would even be able to escape from the car before Karl discovered her.

Senseless rattling … a rock … another rock … and another … why were these cars even called sport utility vehicles, if they shook you up so much?

Lena's head buzzed. The jolting and rattling was giving her a headache. She dared to peek out from under the tarp again, but couldn't see anything. They were far from civilization at this point and only a thin slice of moon shone though the windshield. *We're driving in the shadow of the moonlight,* thought Lena. *Moonlight Shadow* … Lena pulled the tarp over her head again and waited.

Lena had no idea how long they had been driving. Suddenly the car came to a stop. Karl had stalled the engine and he slammed the steering wheel with his palm. Then he turned off the radio and sat there a while. Lena didn't dare to move. If Karl were to look in back now, he would have to notice that there was more than a tarp lying there. *Please don't let him see me!* Lena begged.

"Okay, it's time to bring this to an end," Karl said out

loud and Lena flinched. The tarp rustled quietly, but then Karl opened the car door and got out. Lena realized she had been holding her breath and she quietly breathed out again.

The front car door had been slammed closed and the interior lights went out. Lena waited for a few heartbeats, and then she carefully lifted the tarp.

Karl had left the headlights on. In their light, Lena saw the stocky man walking toward a barn, holding an object that looked like a canister. Little particles flickered spookily in the light of the headlights and threw a thousand little shadows on the wooden wall of the barn. Karl pulled a key out of his pocket and unlocked the barn with it. Without turning around, he disappeared inside.

Lena didn't waste any time. She knew instinctively that it was her only chance. If Karl came back from the barn just now, he would surely discover her – and Lena didn't want to think about what would happen after that. She slipped out from under the tarp, grabbed the car door handle and gently pulled at it. With a soft click, the door opened and the interior light clicked on. Lena froze, briefly startled, but then she remembered what she needed to do. She climbed out of the car and carefully pressed the door closed, and then ducked down behind the car in case Karl had seen the light. But all remained quiet.

Lena breathed in the cold, clear night air. Wherever she was, there wasn't another soul to be seen. What now?

She could stay near the car. Lena gave up her cover and sneaked toward the barn. She pressed herself against the wall across from the door that Karl had used to go inside. But she had to go further, to the back wall of the shed so that she wouldn't be visible from the car.

Pressing one ear against the wall, she listened. Not a single sound disturbed the silence. What if she had been mistaken? What if Shadow wasn't even in this little barn? What if this were just one stop on Karl's trip? Then she'd lose the trail to the stallion, because she'd never make it back to the car.

A noise pierced through the heavy fog that enveloped the stallion. It sounded like the creaking of a wooden door being pushed open. The sounded echoed in the stallion's sensitive ears for a long time until it was just a memory that, like all the other memories, simply dissipated and left the stallion alone in his trance. The world around him was gray and bleak. Although he was sure that his eyes were open, he couldn't recognize anything beyond the thick fog. Instinctively he felt fear rise up in him the closer he got to the surface of the fog. Something told him that he had felt this way before. And that it had almost cost him his life. Still, the fog was too oppressive. It forced the stallion back deep into his trance, where he was held prisoner, far away from any memory and far away from his own will.

Shadow did not feel the second bridle being pulled

over his head and the heavy chain being attached to it. He did not see that the man with the dour face began to frown and almost look sad. He did not notice the canister either, did not smell the acrid stench, was unaware of how Karl distributed the yellow liquid over the straw before pouring the rest over the horse's back.

The stallion fought one more time, as he had fought when the man came to him with the shot. He sensed pending disaster, but the fog mercilessly covered his nostrils, eyes and ears. For Shadow, the fog was an enemy that would not allow its victim to escape with his life a second time.

Karl thoughtlessly threw the canister in a corner and pulled out his lighter. He walked backwards slowly until his back bumped against the door. He looked at the beautiful stallion one last time. *It really is a shame about him*, he thought in a brief moment of doubt. But then he remembered the money that was waiting for him and he shook off the thought. *At least he's checking out without suffering,* he tried to convince himself before flicking his lighter. He threw it into the far corner of the shed. With a hiss, the gasoline raced for the small flame, as if the spark were the only thing alive in there. Soon, very soon, that would be true.

Karl's eyes sparkled in the reflection of the fire. Then he quickly turned around and ran outside into the cold night air.

A hiss penetrated the silence. It was followed by a violent bang, like from an explosion. Karl stormed out of the shed as if the devil himself were chasing him. Lena didn't dare to move. She pressed herself against the back of the bar and hoped that Karl would drive off quickly. A strange heat went through her body. Confused, she took a step back. The air had been so cold a moment ago, but the heat didn't come from the night. Lena swallowed a scream. Flames were coming out of the shed in front of her!

Lena listed as the SUV's engine revved. She waited until the sound of the engine grew distant and then she ran around the shed. Much to her relief, Karl had been in too much of a hurry to lock the door. Lena took a deep breath. She tore the door open and bounced back. The floor of the barn was completely covered in hay, which was ablaze. Lena had to cough so hard that she ran back into the dark to fill her lungs with the clear night air.

Shadow! The thought shot into her head. No doubt, the stallion had to be in the barn. But why wasn't he making any noise? No whinny, no stomping with his hooves, nothing. Lena knew there was only one way to rescue the stallion. She had to go into the shed.

"Leeeenaaaaaa!"

Britta and Ellie had searched the entire courtyard without finding even the slightest sign of their friend.

Mr. Hansen had gone through the stable three times, while both policemen checked the adjoining buildings with Sandra and Mrs. Von Bernheim. The result was staggering; it was as if Lena had been swallowed up by the earth!

The first stars twinkled in the early evening sky as the small group met up again under the big chestnut tree in the courtyard. The taller policeman scratched his head thoughtfully.

"Let's look at this logically. The girl came here with you, which means that she was here at the farm. Now she's gone, but all of us are still here. How could she have left?"

"Maybe she's locked in somewhere? Like in the barn or something?"

"Impossible," surmised the shorter policeman. "Otherwise she would have responded to our calls. I believe that she isn't here any more. Mrs. Von Bernheim, had anyone left the farm in the last half hour? Maybe with an automobile?"

The elegant woman's face turned as white as the light of the moon. She looked aghast and stared at the policeman for a few seconds, before catching herself again. She pursed her lips. "Hmm, hard to say. My employees come and go as they please. Hansen, did you notice anything?"

The long-haired man shrugged his shoulders. "It's

possible that I heard a car, but it could have been a rider, or a stable hand, or …"

"Alright already," sighed the shorter policeman. "Did the girl have a cell phone with her?"

Britta pulled out her own phone and called Lena's number. It rang twice, before a child's voice answered it.

"Larry Bergman!"

"Larry – oh, hi, it's Britta! Where are you? Is Lena there with you?" As she finished saying that she realized how absurd her question had been.

"No, but I have her phone!"

Britta lowered her phone and shook her head wordlessly.

"That just can't be," groaned Sandra. She glanced at her wristwatch, sighed and reached out her hand for the phone.

"Hello? May I speak with your parents, please? Yes, I'm a friend of Lena's."

Ellie pushed herself against Britta's side. In her thin jacket she shivered like a dry branch. And not just because it was cold, she guessed.

The taller policeman bent down to his car and fumbled for his radio receiver. The other could hear him speaking with his colleagues. Then he handed the girls the mouthpiece and asked them to describe Lena.

Sandra's face looked upset, as if it were her own daughter who had gone missing.

"Good evening, Mr. Bergman, this is Sandra. Yes,

something happened. Please stay calm, no, not a car accident … Well, I'm not sure how to explain it … We don't really know ourselves. Lena has disappeared …"

An acrid stench came from the shed and mixed with the clear night air. It smelled like a gas station – gasoline! Lena turned away and took a deep breath. *Just don't contemplate things, don't think any rational thoughts now.* She had no choice. She had to go in there, had to see if the horse was in the shed!

With one fast movement, Lena pulled her beloved Icelandic sweater over her head and pressed the thick wool in front of her face so that she could see out of it. Then she held her breath and entered the burning barn.

The heat came at her with such force that Lena staggered and nearly tripped over a burning log. She had to force herself not to breathe by pure force of will. She pressed her sweater closer to her face, and then groped her way along the wooden wall.

The smoke burned her eyes and made it nearly impossible to make out anything. Lena blinked intensely and restrained the impulse to run away from the heat that grew more intense. Another beam crashed to the ground and left behind a brief shimmer of clear air. In that second she saw him.

Oh no! Shadow! Lena stopped thinking. She lunged forwards without paying attention to the beams that were crashing down. After a few steps she was standing next to the stallion, but he wasn't moving! Lena felt the tears in her eyes, but they didn't come from the biting smoke around her. Shadow looked as if he were dead.

I have to do something to get him out of here, Lena thought suddenly. She saw that the stallion was bound to the walls of the shed with two thick chains. As hard as she tried, she couldn't disconnect them. Full of panic, Lena noticed herself running out of air. She had to get out, had to breathe! What should she do? Then she recognized her mistake. The chains weren't the problem – all she had to do was take off the bridle! With her free hand she felt for the catch and then the first bridle fell to the ground, where the flames greedily engulfed it. The second bridle was opened just as quickly and the stallion was free. But why didn't he move? Lena realized with desperation that she couldn't hold her breath any longer and did the only thing that occurred to her in that moment – with her hand open, she gave the horse's nose a sharp slap.

And then it was as if the stallion was awakened from a long nap. He shook his mane, carefully turned his head and looked Lena directly in the eyes. Suddenly it seemed as if his senses had also awakened and he emitted a frightened whinny.

Lena couldn't take it any longer. She pressed herself tightly against the only wall in the shed that wasn't in flames yet and felt her way along the wall until she reached the door. Like a drowning person finally feeling the ground under her feet again, she staggered into the open air and gasped the fresh night air. When she felt something move next to her, she turned her head and saw with relief that the stallion had followed her.

"Shadow, oh my sweet horse – oh my goodness!"

The stallion had walked out through the fire. He was so dazed that there was only one thing he could do, namely to follow the girl. The girl who had chased away the fog and brought him back to life. He didn't know that his back was drenched with gasoline and that it had attracted the flames like a magnet.

Lena screamed and beat Shadow's back with her Icelandic sweater. The flames ate through the thick wool, but could not win against it. When all that was left of the sweater was just bits and pieces, Lena pulled it off of the stallion's back and leaned, shivering against his black flank. She alternated between laughing and crying. When she looked back, the small barn was completely ablaze.

"We didn't get out of there a minute too soon!" Lena whispered, awestruck. She couldn't believe what had just happened. Overcome, she stroked the stallion along his neck and tried to calm down her own gasping. Now that the shock was receding, she felt her knees go soft.

If I hadn't gotten into Karl's car … Lena hardly noticed the tears of relief that ran down her cheeks. She didn't want to think that thought to its natural conclusion!

The morning was colored by a golden light, although the sun was still low in the sky. An icy wind blew across the meadows and fields.

Chilled, Lena stood up. She had tried to catch a little sleep underneath a big chestnut tree, but the cold night air and lack of protection from her warm sweater prevented her from closing her eyes at all. The cold numbed her arms and legs; still she savored the feeling. Every muscle that ached, every pain she felt, told her that she was still alive, she and the beautiful black stallion that stood next to her as though her were standing guard over her.

Lena had left the burning barn far behind her in the night. She walked until she couldn't see the light of the fire anymore.

Somewhere along the way her exhausted legs gave out from under her and Lena leaned helplessly against a tree and stayed there, her chilled arms wrapped around her legs until the dawn.

Shadow stayed with her the entire time. Because Lena didn't have a bridle for him she just let him walk freely. As she shook her stiff limbs, he snorted and came over to her to blow his warm breath in her face.

The stallion's back looked awful. Lena knew that she had saved his life with her Icelandic sweater, but the wounds would take time to heal. They wouldn't disappear as easily as they had the last time.

Lena gently stroked his soft nose. *Think of what people are willing to do just to make a profit on a horse,* she thought contemptuously. *I don't want to ride in any more tournaments. I will never use a horse again to achieve something that's only for me.*

Lena didn't know how long she had been roaming around. Her stomach growled, she felt dirty and still smelled the acrid smoke on her clothes. She kept walking in one direction clear across the meadows and harvested fields. She paid no attention to paths and every time she looked over her shoulder, she got a warm feeling in her stomach to see that Shadow was still following her.

The red roof of the old farmhouse looked like a toy when it first appeared on the horizon. Lena blinked and shaded her eyes with one hand from the low sun. As she got closer, she noticed other houses that formed a little village. A wide street led through the village and, at the other end, disappeared into the woods.

Lena headed straight for the farmhouse with the red roof. To her it felt as if this house was calling to her, leading her back into civilization across fields and meadows like a lighthouse. Shadow stopped just before the driveway of the small farm and stood rooted to the spot, flaring his nostrils. Lena wanted to encourage him along, but then she saw the shed. It was made of wood and, judging by the noises that emanated from it, housed the farm's chickens and geese. At first glance it looked just like the shed that had been consumed last night by a sea of flames. Of course – Shadow wouldn't want to get near a shed like that any time soon.

Lena looked around. In the cowshed she heard the clanking of milk pails. She quickly smoothed her mussed hair and wiped as much of the soot from her face as she could. Then she slowly walked through the open barn door.

The farmer's wife was so alarmed that she almost dropped her pail when she saw the girl.

I must look pretty bad, thought Lena in confusion. The warm stable had a strange effect on her...

"Good heavens, child! What happened to you?"

"Oh, could I please use your phone to call the police? My name is Lena Bergman, I, the horse..." Lena didn't get beyond that. Suddenly everything went black. The last thing she saw was the farmer's wife lunging toward her. Then she fainted, collapsing onto a pile of hay.

When Lena came to, she was wrapped in a soft blanket, nestled in the hay. She heard the cows mooing around her and carefully sat up. Next to her sat a small, scraggly farm dog that wagged his tail happily at her.

"It seems our guest finally woke up, right Denny?" The farmer's wife appeared in the doorway with a cup of steaming hot milk in her hand. "Here, this will bring you back to life," she smiled as she reached the cup to Lena.

The warm milk was good and Lena drank it in big gulps.

"By the way, Officer Knoll told me to give you his best," the farmer's wife continued. "They knew right away who you were when I called the police station. I'm supposed to keep an eye on you and make sure you don't disappear again!"

Lena wrapped her hands around the cup. "Thanks a lot. You're so kind to me! I didn't run away, you know – I had to save a friend's life. Oh," Lena peeled back the blanket and stood up. "The horse that came here with me. Where is he?"

"He's standing out there in our field. I wanted to lure him but he wasn't interested in me. Then I put out some hay for him, but he just stood there and stared at the barn. I think he'd like for you to come out."

Lena's face began to brighten. Shadow had really waited for her!

The stallion perked his ears as Lena walked out into the sunlight. He walked over to her and let her stroke and scratch him. He stood there for a while, with his head leaning against Lena's shoulder. In the bright sunlight his back looked worse than it had at dawn. Lena grabbed a handful of hay and took a sniff. It smelled wonderful, and as though he had read her mind, Shadow's nostrils flared. Lena pretended that she wanted to taste the hay and Shadow's mouth came closer to her face. Then she laughed quietly and offered the stallion his breakfast, served on her palm. The stallion ate hungrily, as if he hadn't had a bite in days.

"Your friend could use a little of my special ointment. It's especially good on open wounds." Lena observed how the farmer's wife fearlessly approached the stallion. With a trained hand, she applied the thick white gel to Shadow's back. The ointment really did seem to have a calming effect, because Shadow didn't move an inch during the entire procedure.

By the time the police arrived, Lena had told her rescuer the entire unbelievable story.

The contingent of cars that swarmed through the village half an hour later hardly found enough space to park at the small farm. Suddenly, the entire yard was full of people talking in a cacophony of voices.

"Lena! Oh good heavens, Lena, what happened to you?"

"You found Shadow! Oh no, what's wrong with him?"

"We were afraid someone had kidnapped you!"

Lena laughed and raised her hands to hold everyone back. She felt strange now that everything was over, like after waking up from a crazy dream. But the rough blanket around her shoulders and the soot in her face reminded her of the truth.

Mrs. Bergman's eyes were red. She wrapped her arms tightly around her daughter. Larry clung to his father's hand and looked at his sister with an expression of awe.

"I'd like to file a complaint," Lena looked over at the thin woman who was standing next to a long-haired man, looking completely out of place at the small farm. No doubt, that had to be Mrs. Von Bernheim! "A complaint regarding attempted insurance fraud and attempted horse murder."

The two policemen exchanged a look of surprise. "And who are you accusing of this?"

"I don't know his full name," said Lena grimly, "but I know who he works for!"

Lena described how she overheard the conversation in the stable and subsequently rode in Karl's car covered by the tarp. Her mother slapped her hand to her mouth in shock as she heard what happened next.

Mrs. Von Bernheim took a step forward. "I can assure you that I have no idea..."

"Are you absolutely certain?" the taller policeman interrupted her and turned to Lena. "After all, you couldn't see Mrs. Von Bernheim from inside the box."

"I recognize her voice, though," Lena nodded "Besides, Shadow's kidnapper called her by name!"

"That is just outrageous," exclaimed Mrs. Von Bernheim. "You aren't really going to buy into this girl's horror stories. Karl will attest that absolutely none of this is true."

"Who is this Karl, anyway?" the shorter policeman asked.

"He works as a stable hand and sometimes helps out around the property," the long-haired man interjected.

"And he picked up Shadow," Lena called out. "He was wearing a hat, though, so that we wouldn't recognize him later!"

"Then he's probably the one who originally stole the stallion – under orders from this lady here!"

The shorter policeman took out his notebook and began furiously taking notes.

"What I don't understand is how the horse wound up with you. Karl couldn't have just let it go in the woods."

"It got away from him," grunted Mrs. Von Bernheim angrily. "This incompetent fool isn't even capable of tying up a horse in a barn!"

"Ah, and you knew about that," concluded the taller policemen in passing.

Stunned, the long-haired man stared at his employer. "How could you allow that to happen!"

"Because he was good for nothing," screeched Mrs. Von Bernheim angrily. "This animal cost me huge sums of money and then turned stubborn when it came to winning something. I know that he can jump; that's why I bought him. But this beast just didn't want to!"

Lena suddenly had to think of the old farmer who had given her the saddle. Hadn't he said something similar? *If the horse doesn't enjoy jumping, then you'll never win.*

"But Shadow had fun jumping," she mumbled to herself. "He just didn't want to do it for you!"

"I don't understand why Shadow didn't resist," Britta

said. "He just strolled into the trailer with Karl and then let himself be tied up in the shed." She quickly looked over to Lena. "In the garden he never wanted to go anywhere near our little shed, remember?"

"Karl probably drugged him," the long-haired man suggested. "Probably gave him something to eat when you weren't paying attention."

"Sugar cubes!" Lena saw the fat fingers again in her mind's eye. "Oh my gosh!"

The taller policeman raised his hands. "Okay, that's enough for me. Mrs. Von Bernheim, you are under arrest for serious cruelty to animals and attempted insurance fraud."

His colleague handed the report he had been writing over to Lena's parents for their signature.

"I'll send a car out immediately to arrest this Karl fellow."

"Just a minute!" Lena felt that the time had come. A decision would have to be made. She stepped forward and looked at the two policemen with a serious expression on her face.

"What will happen now with Shadow ... I mean, with Black Diamond?"

The shorter policeman looked surprised, as if the thought hadn't yet occurred to him. "He'll probably be auctioned off," he said after thinking it over. "Along with all the other horses in the Von Bernheim stables."

"You wouldn't dare!" screamed Mrs. Von Bernheim hysterically. "Hansen, do something!"

But her head groom had his arms crossed across his chest and shook his head defiantly.

Lena felt her eyes fill with tears. She swallowed and tried not to let her despair show. Would she lose Shadow again? That just couldn't happen! "Couldn't we buy him?" She looked at her parents beseechingly.

"But Lena," sighed Mrs. Bergman. "We don't have room for a horse."

"But we could board him at the riding school!"

"And who is supposed to pay for all that? I'm sorry, Lena, but it's just not possible."

In all that time, no one had taken note of Sandra, who was standing next to Shadow and carefully inspecting him. As she walked back to the group, her shadow preceded her. "I'd like to buy the stallion," she said casually, as if it were the most normal thing in the world.

"What?" Lena practically shouted for joy. "That would be wonderful!"

"You know I've got a weakness for sensitive horses," Sandra shrugged her shoulders. "Besides, he'd be a terrific father for my mare Misty's future foals!"

"And what would you do with Shadow … uh, Black Diamond?" Britta asked excitedly.

Sandra smiled. "First of all, he'll get a new name. One that fits better with his new life. What do you think, *Moonlight Shadow*?" She stroked the black stallion lovingly along his neck, "And then you'll all have to help me find a new place for him to stay. A stallion can't live at the riding school."

"We could put up flyers," Britta offered right away.

"Or we could build a stable for him ourselves," Ellie said eagerly.

"In a pinch he could go back to his old home," laughed Lena. "Then he'd just have to live a while longer in the woodland garden."

Sandra smiled gratefully. "And of course I'd need a horse caretaker for him. Or better yet two…" Then she turned to the policemen, looking serious. "What do you think, is my intent to purchase the stallion realistic?"

"You mean, will you get him? Well," the shorter policeman scratched his chin, crooked his neck and looked up into the fall sky, as if he had to think hard about the question. Then he smiled, "I think I can take care of that."

Finally, she had her answer! Lena cheered with all of the others. She alternated hugs between Sandra, Britta, her parents and Ellie. Even the friendly farmer's wife got a big hug from everyone.

Over the loud and happy voices they suddenly heard the miserable yowling of a dog. Lena gave a start because she recognized that voice only too well.

Baloo had been tied up at a pole so that he wouldn't have to wait in the car for too long. His family always wanted the best for him, but Baloo seemed terribly afraid that he was being abandoned permanently. His howling sounded heartbreaking.

"Oh, my little Baloo!" Lena ran over to the dog and wrapped her arms around his neck. Baloo joyfully licked her face.

"You don't need to be afraid. We're taking you home again – both of you!"

Lena untied her dog and walked over to the stallion. Slowly, acting as if it was costing him all of his doggie courage, Baloo slinked along behind her. He stood next to Lena and carefully wagged his tail. Shadow lowered his head and snorted quietly. Baloo was startled, but he stayed where he was. He gently licked the stallion's nose before dashing behind Lena for safety.

Lena laughed spiritedly.

"Did you see that? Now Shadow really does belong to us!"